ALWAYS FAITHFUL

ALWAYS FAITHFUL

ISABELLA

SAPPHIRE BOOKS

SALINAS, CALIFORNIA

Sapphire Books
Salinas, CA 93912
www.sapphirebooks.com

Printed in the United States of America
First Edition – August 2010

Acknowledgements

This book is dedicated to the women who served, are serving, and will serve our country with honor, valor and dignity. May we never forget that women die in conflict, too. Your selflessness is a constant inspiration to me. To my wife, thank you for your service, without it, we would never have met.

Thank you to the beta readers; Ilene, Probingreality, and Lee. Your feedback was invaluable. This book wouldn't be possible without the help of Victoria. Thank you for the lessons learned, the friendship during the process and the reminder that it's a craft.

To the one woman in my life who has brought me more joy than I will ever be able to give her. You are my inspiration for those things that I find joy in. I love you, *mi amor, eres mi vida.*

To my sons who have helped craft the person I am today. I love you more than words could ever convey.

CHAPTER ONE

God, how she hated this part of her job. Major Nichol Caldwell looked at her reflection in the mirror, smoothed a few strands of brown hair into place, and adjusted her uniform for the last time before leaving her office. She hated doing "informs", the term she'd given to the process of calling on family members to inform them of a loved one killed or lost in Iraq.

The Chaplain was waiting outside her office. "Ready Major?"

"As ready as I ever am in this situation, Father. This is the worst part of my job. No matter how many I do, I'm never prepared for them."

"You know, of all the officers who've accompanied me on these, you have been the most understanding and supportive. Remember, God doesn't tell us why he is testing our courage. We just have to do what we can for our fellow soldiers and their families during their time of need." He placed a kindly hand on her shoulder before heading to the car.

Nic didn't want to tell the priest that she had lost her faith a long time ago. No, now wasn't the time for a philosophical debate on whether God even existed and if so, how could he let those so brave die so needlessly. They'd debated that many times in the past and she didn't have the energy to spar with him today.

She knew the dead officer's family fairly well. Captain Mike Monroe had been two years behind her in ROTC and they'd taken a few engineering classes together, drilled together, and socialized with some of the same people in college. ROTC was a small community, in general, and on a college campus it was even smaller. She and Mike went through flight school at the same time. Even though he was in an attack unit and she was in a medivac unit, they were still in aviation and aviation was a tight group. She wouldn't say they were close, but she knew him well enough to feel sick to her stomach at his death. Mike left behind a little girl who would never know her father and wouldn't understand what was happening. Maybe that was a blessing in disguise. Nic had met Claire, Mike's widow, at a few social events on the base. She was a beautiful woman and Mike was a lucky man, *was* being the operative word. Now she had to go and turn Claire's world upside down, shattering her dreams for the future.

Every house on the base at Camp Pendleton looked the same from the outside. Standard military housing with no frills and no big swimming pools in the backyards. The buildings ran together, ugly beige or grey paint blending together like the desert land they sat on, marked as separate by the occasional fence that penned in the obligatory dog. Here the rules were clear. Mow your lawn, watch how fast you drive, and never, ever, let your kids run the streets. These habits made for quiet neighborhoods that were simple and bland without a hint about the sacrifices the families made to be a part of these tight neighborhoods.

When she pulled up to the house, Nic knew the neighbors would be watching. They were always watching. It was part of some implied military family code. For that very reason crime was low in military housing. It was a small bonus to be living with like-minded people. Nic got out of her car and waited for the Chaplain to join her. *Man this sucks.* Why did she have to pull this duty when she got back from Iraq? Why couldn't she just fly a desk like so many of her other counterparts who had been wounded? Oh, right. She *was* flying a desk and her desk flights included death notifications.

She knocked on the door with a cute little sign announcing who lived at this residence. When no one answered she looked over at the carport and noticed the tan sedan parked in the driveway. Perhaps Claire Monroe was taking a nap or she was over at a neighbor's house. Nic knocked harder, rattling the wooden sign on the door.

"Be right there." The door opened slowly and Claire Monroe appeared in the doorway, the sun backlighting her slender figure and obscuring her features. "Good Morning. What can I do for...?" She looked from Nic to the Chaplain as the words died on her lips. "No— no. Oh, God. Please no. Go away. You're at the wrong house. Please, please, tell me you're at the wrong house. Please—" Claire turned towards the house, as though by shutting the door she would shut out the impending news.

"Mrs. Monroe, please—" Nic's voice cracked as she followed the unofficial "script" for these occasions. "May we come inside and tell you why we're here?"

"I know why you're here. You're here to tell me that Mike isn't coming home, aren't you, Major? You're here to tell me that the Corps is sorry for my loss and that Mike died a hero. Right?" Claire was practically screaming now. "Answer me, Major."

All Nic could do was look at her spit-shined shoes and wish she were somewhere else. "Yes ma'am. Can we go inside now, Mrs. Monroe? Father O'Rielly and I are here to help in any way we can, to give you support, and to tell you what we know about what happened in Iraq."

The Chaplain put a hand on Claire's shoulder. "Please, Mrs. Monroe, can we come in?"

Nic watched tears stream down Claire's face. She despised what this war was doing to families all over the United States. Here she was to tell another family how their loved one had died a hero, in a war they were never going to win. In the beginning, she had believed in the war, but as it continued, she had witnessed the devastation first hand and it angered her. She wondered how a commander-in-chief, who had only served in the National Guard, could send American troops in to win something that he knew damn well wasn't winnable. For a brief moment, Nic thought of her own crew and wondered how their families were doing. She made it a point to keep in touch, but it had been weeks since she had talked to any of the families. She didn't want them to think they were forgotten or that their sacrifice was for nothing. A sob pulled Nic back to reality. *God, I hate this job*, she thought for the third time in as many minutes.

"Mrs. Monroe, I'm so sorry for your loss. I know that sounds trite, but if there is anything I can do right now, please let me know," Nic said softly.

"Can you bring back my husband, Major? Can you do that for me? Otherwise there is nothing you can do to help me and my daughter." Nic watched, as a sudden realization seemed to hit Claire. "Oh God. How will I tell Grace that her dad isn't coming home? Oh God!" Claire crumpled to her knees, burying her face in her hands as she wept uncontrollably. "How will I ever tell her?"

Right at that moment, one of Mrs. Monroe's neighbors came out of the cookie cutter house next door and walked over. "Claire, I'm so sorry. Come on. Let's go inside, honey." Turning, she extended her hand and introduced herself. "Good morning Officers. I'm Claire's neighbor, Debbie Rouch. Let's get Claire inside and see what we can do to make her comfortable."

Nic felt helpless as she shook the hand of another military wife who knew she could be in Claire's shoes at any time. Nic tried to help Claire up, but she was like a rag doll lacking any internal structure. So Nic gently lifted Claire into her arms and carried the woman inside. When Nic placed her on the couch, she noticed Claire's expression had changed from anger to a hollow mask, utterly devoid of emotion.

She had seen soldiers who had their whole lives ahead of them die. Futures snuffed out like a flame in a hurricane. The stories were usually the same. A soldier is deployed to Iraq, goes out on a routine mission and a bomb takes out half the squad. Those, who survived were sometimes wounded so badly that they wished they were dead. Then they came home to families so happy they'd survived, no one cared what condition they were in, just as long as they'd come home, because the alternative was worse.

Nic watched as Debbie Rouch put her arm around Claire's shoulders and gently rocked Claire like a child needing comforting. Nic knew the pain was so great that nothing would penetrate Claire's emotional fog for days, but when it finally did, her grief would reach into her soul, claiming whatever it could.

Nic had been there often in the past three months. In fact, she was starting to question whether she should stay in the Corps. The loss of her crew was hard on her and it was one of the reasons she was stateside at the base in San Diego doing informs. She wasn't in a hurry to be redeployed as so many of her fellow pilots were after recovery. Nic relived the accident every day she drove by the airfield on her way to work, or every time she had to see a family and inform them of the loss of a loved one. Moreover, she relived it every time she looked at her scars.

Today was just a little different, because this time Nic knew this inform. Today she had to tell the wife of an acquaintance that she must wake up alone tomorrow. Something Claire had done a hundred times since her husband's deployment. However, from this time on it would be a permanent way of life. All the Corps could offer was some counseling, a polite thank you from the President of the United States, a life insurance policy of four hundred thousand dollars, thirty days to vacate family housing, and the offer to move her household goods to a permanent residence, wherever that may be.

Nic felt a gentle hand on her shoulder and looked up to see the Chaplain staring down at her. "I'm sorry, Father. What did you say?"

"I asked if it would be possible for you to come by and check on Mrs. Monroe later. Since you two seem to have some history together." He searched Nic's face. "In fact, would you mind lending a hand to Mrs. Monroe during this difficult time, perhaps helping her get Mike's affairs in order? I know it is a little out of the ordinary, but Claire was just telling me she doesn't have family close by. Only a friend who won't be able to come immediately and it will be a few days before Mike's family can get here." Pausing, he looked back at Claire and added, "I'm sure Mike would appreciate it, too."

"Father, I don't know if that's such a good idea. Wouldn't it be better to have someone around who won't remind her of Mike?"

The Chaplain shrugged off her concerns. "Right now, she doesn't have anyone who knows the system as well as you do. We have personnel who could advise her—but they're strangers, you were a friend of her husband's. She might be able to confide and grieve with you, whereas that would likely prove harder with a stranger."

"Fine," she said. "I'll do what I can."

She received a look of relief from Mrs. Rouch, who had made a cup of coffee for Claire and was standing close enough to listen to their conversation. Claire sat on the couch, her gaze unfocused. She sipped her drink automatically, clearly lost in her own stunned memories.

"I think you can help more than you know," the Chaplain said. "Remember, as someone much older than me said, 'What doesn't kill us makes us stronger.' You've been through a lot yourself. I'm sure you can lend some of your strength and support to Mrs. Monroe."

Nic nodded silently. *Okay, but how do I help her with her pain when I don't know how to deal with my own?*

CHAPTER TWO

Claire looked around the room and saw a few wives whispering and wiping their eyes. They looked at her with the same look she had given other wives who had lost their husbands; disbelief and relief mixed with a dose of pity. She saw Chaplain O'Rielly and Major Caldwell talking and she wondered if she would ever be able to look at that uniform the same way again. Mike looked so smart in his uniform. It transformed him the minute he put it on. He had a military bearing about him, a pride that she was sure only someone who wore the uniform understood. He had told her many times how proud he was to serve his country and he had died for that very honor.

Once the word got out, every wife in Mike's unit stopped by to see if she could help in some way.

Claire felt a hand on her shoulder. "Claire, I am so sorry for your loss. Is there anything I can do to help? Maybe I can take Grace for a while?"

Turning into the touch Claire reached up and patted the hand on her shoulder. "Thank you, Gail. There isn't really anything I need right now."

"Claire, you know we're here for you," said another wife wiping her eyes, "and you know that you can call one of us anytime of the day or night, honey."

"Thanks, Shirley, I appreciate that. Really I do."

Claire knew they meant well, but she couldn't tell them how they could help even if she wanted to. The constant talking around her made her head buzz. She was in a fog that deepened the longer everyone stayed. She couldn't focus. She couldn't think. She couldn't function with everyone around. After what seemed like hours, Claire finally found the strength to ask everyone to leave. She needed to be alone with her daughter. She wanted time to think about what had just happened and how she was going to explain to Grace that her daddy wasn't coming home, ever.

"Thanks again everyone for the food and everything," Claire said as she watched the wives leave.

"Let us know when the funeral is Claire," someone in the group said.

"I will. Thank you again." Closing the door, Claire leaned against it for support.

She thought about her daughter and started to cry again, not for herself but for Grace. She slid down the door and hugged her knees to her chest. Grace adored her dad and Mike adored her. She cried harder when she realized that Mike would never see Grace grow up to be a beautiful woman, walk her down the aisle for her wedding, or bounce his grandchildren on his knee. Regardless of the type of relationship she and Mike had, he was a devoted father. He doted on Grace and it was clear that she had him wrapped around her little finger. In fact, Claire would often raise her little pinky, wiggling it at Mike when he gave in to Grace during one of her tantrums. Laughing, Mike would always say, "Hey, she is the best thing I have ever done in my life, and I refuse to be the bad guy. Besides, that's your job, right?" Although it would draw a mock grunt of disgust from his wife, she would always smile at how much he loved being a dad.

Claire walked to her daughter's room and sat in

the rocker Mike had bought her when she had Grace. She watched Grace sleep, and wondered how much a three-year-old little girl would understand what happened to her father. She thought about how different their life would be now that Mike was gone. Did he suffer? Did he know what was happening or did it happen so fast that he didn't know what hit him?

She thought about Mike's family. They were a tight-knit group, the kind of family Claire wished she had growing up. They were close and happy, always looking out for each other. Mike's mom irritated Claire sometimes, but Claire understood that she only wanted the best for Mike. It was something she could relate to now as she looked at Grace, but as close as Mike and his family were, he had kept a secret from them. One, Claire would now have to keep no matter what happened. It was something she was glad she could do for Mike, especially now. The past didn't matter as much as it had two days ago, and she had to look towards the future-one without Mike.

She thought about Mike, and guilt started to eat at Claire. Had she been a good wife? Had she made him happy, at least in the ways that mattered to Mike? She did all the "wifely" duties she thought she was supposed to. From the outside they were the ideal military family.

Grace started to stir and Claire was at her side immediately, picking her up and hugging her. Grace laid her head on her mother's shoulder and Claire stroked her short, wispy hair. There was no denying Grace was Mike's, she had his big blue eyes and his full lips.

"She'll be a heart-breaker," Mike often said when he looked at his daughter. He joked he would be the type of parent that would welcome his daughter's boyfriends while he was cleaning his shotgun. "Just to start the relationship off right," he would joke.

"Oh honey," whispered Claire as she rocked her little girl. Claire looked into her daughter's eyes and choked back a sob.

"It's okay Mommy. I take care of you," Grace said as she wiped a tear from her mom's face. Claire cried harder as she realized she had to tell her daughter something even she couldn't believe yet. *Damnit. How could Mike do this to us? Damn him, damn him, damn it all to hell. She sat back down in the rocker with her daughter held tightly against her.*

###

Nic sat at her desk, her head in her hands, running her fingers through her hair as she wondered what she had gotten herself into. She was still struggling with her own scars from Iraq and now she had to deal with helping a family start the process of getting through their own ordeal. Claire Monroe had to process out of military housing in thirty days and then she would be with her own family and working through her issues with them. Thirty days wasn't that long. Nic had been back almost three months, although sometimes it seemed like forever. Other times, it felt like only yesterday.

Months had passed since her medivac helicopter went down in Iraq. Her first few weeks were spent in the hospital as they repaired her destroyed body, then the next few weeks were spent in rehab as she learned to walk again. She had been told the burns and grafts would take time to heal, and the hospital staff had been adamant about maintaining a daily regiment of workouts. The works outs helped her body to heal, but not her mind. The sound of the crash then bodies and burning wreckage everywhere still haunted her. Everyday she thought about her friends who had died, and every day she wondered. 'Why me? Why did I survive and not Jack, who had a wife and three kids? Or the navigator Craig who had just married his high school sweetheart?' She thought about them, about their families and how they were coping with their loss. She thought about it all, everyday.

Nic was still seeing a doctor weekly for her injuries, and to top it all off they were still making her see a shrink. "Just to make sure everything is fine upstairs." Bullshit. They wanted to make sure she wasn't some loose cannon who would freak out at any minute and go shooting up the place. She had heard about the combat stress many of the soldiers were coming home with, and how some of the soldiers were killing their spouses and themselves because they couldn't deal with life stateside. Well, that wasn't her. She knew she had better coping skills than that. After the crap she'd dealt with in her childhood, she could handle anything. She had chosen the Marine Corps to prove to everyone she'd ever known that she could take anything that came her way.

Looking down at her watch and noting the time she got up, put her hair back in a bun, and hefted her workout bag onto her shoulder. A good hour on the weights, more than a few laps in the pool, and then the sauna. Her gym workouts not only kept her sane, but also the exertion helped relax her and gave her the time and space she needed to think things through. She would work out her emotions in private, without a shrink staring at her waiting for her to make some revelation she didn't feel. When she was in Bethesda after the crash, she practically came unglued at first, because she wasn't able to get up off the bed, let alone walk. It hadn't taken her long after her surgeries to get to the point of being able to not only sit up, but also to get up and walk without help. She made it through, pushing the emotional pain out of her mind once again as she had done so many other times before. *You're here, you survived and you have a future ahead of you, whether you like it or not.*

"Hey handsome! Back so soon?"

"Hey Trevor. Talk like that might get ya a date. Just not with me," she said, winking at the gym attendant.

"Yeah, you officers are all alike. No guts no glory," Trevor said as he swiped her ID card.

"Yeah, well I don't want to go to the brig for fraternizing, and trust me, I'm not your type. Now that blonde over there," Nic said pointing to a woman running on the treadmill, "she looks like your type. Why don't you give her a try?"

"Already did. She shot me down, too." Trevor rested his head on his hands as he watched the woman running on the treadmill.

"Well don't give up hope. I'm sure you'll find someone in this shit hole. Chicks dig a guy in uniform."

An hour later she was sweating so much that her T-shirt was sticking to her body like a second skin. She often lost track of time when she worked out, getting into a zone where she felt intensely alive, her heart pounding as she pushed herself. At times she worked to excess, to the point where she almost couldn't get up because her muscles were so fatigued. She knew she could keep up with the best of the best on their P.T. tests, often lapping some of the younger males. At almost six feet, she was an imposing figure with broad shoulders, narrow hips, and well-defined arms and legs, but when she looked in the mirror, all she saw was that weak, wounded soldier at Bethesda. Maybe *that* was why she was still seeing the shrink.

Nic reached for the tingling scar on her back as she made her way to the locker room to finish her workout. It was itching from the sweat, and her soaked T-shirt rubbing against it was a constant reminder of everything she had lost in Iraq. She changed into her swimsuit and continued on to the pool to do her normal thirty laps. Nic rinsed out her swim goggles and couldn't help but check out a woman sitting on the edge of the pool. She was talking to a slim, pale guy in a Speedo who was leaning over laughing.

Yuk dude, ditch the Speedo, thought Nic as she watched the woman throw her head back as she laughed. *You could do so much better than Mr. Pasty.*

Nic watched for a second too long and was caught looking. Smiling and arching an eyebrow, the woman stared back at Nic. Her eyes roamed up and down Nic's body and then back to Nic's eyes.

Did she just wink at me? Nic watched the woman slide the tip of her index finger into her parted lips and bite it.

"Hey, earth to Theresa," Mr. Pasty said, snapping his fingers in front of the woman's face. "Hey, we need to get back to the office."

Nic took the opportunity to don her goggles and plunge into the water. She started to stroke the warm water when she caught Theresa watching her as she walked along the side of the pool to the locker room, her ass firm under her black swimsuit. Pulling up Nic saw Theresa take one last look at her and wave. Nic politely waved back and smiled before returning to her laps. She grinned at the simple and unexpected flirtation before putting it out of her mind and ducking beneath the heavily chlorinated water. Each long stroke strained her already tired shoulders. Her arms shook with fatigue when she finally stopped. Pulling herself up on the side of the pool, she took a long deep breath. This was exactly what she had needed to get her mind off her last inform.

After showering, Nic walked to the mirror and wiped off the steam that had collected during her shower. She assessed her reflection before she brushed her hair. At least the accident hadn't left any facial injuries, thanks to her flight helmet. Nevertheless, when she looked at her green eyes they looked different, almost as if someone else was looking back at her.

She finished drying off, applied the bandages to her scars and pulled the tight T-shirt over her broad shoulders. It hugged her body, accentuating her full breasts and hard abs. If there was one thing Nic liked, it was her body in tight clothes. She worked out hard and she wasn't about to hide the results with baggy sweats or clothes. She pulled her low-slung jeans over her narrow hips, tucked her T-shirt in and slipped into her favorite boots. She packed her bag and slung it over her shoulder, feeling a sting when it hit her back. It was getting better. It wasn't as painful as it had been in the beginning when she would sling her bag, slapping it against her back without thinking and causing excruciating pain. These were small victories on her way to a full recovery and a normal life.

She strode out of the gym and over to her Yamaha, her other stress reliever. She had ridden a motorcycle since she was a kid, but after her crash, she had to wait until the doctors okayed her to ride. If they found out she was riding without being cleared she could be court-martialed since she was *still* government property, as she was often reminded.

Nic had never resented that equation until Iraq. She had never questioned the debt she owed her country, she knew what she was signing on for when she joined the Marine Corps. She wanted a college education, discipline, respect and a chance to serve her country. She knew her family would never pay for her to go to college so she hit up her Uncle Sam, who was more than willing to help her out as long as she knew the rules.

Until now, her life seemed to make sense. But somewhere between the sickening sound of her helicopter exploding and those long days in her bed at Bethesda, she'd lost that certainty. Her bike rumbled just loud enough to make her heart vibrate and tickle her center as she eased the chrome horse out of the parking space to the exit. She loved the freedom the bike gave her. It was like nothing she ever felt in anything else she did, not flying a helicopter, driving a sports car or the high she got from pumping weights. The only thing that came close was the pre-orgasmic shudder she had when she made love to a woman.

Luckily, traffic was light and she wasn't in a hurry to get home to an empty apartment or worse, another inform. Nic weaved in and out of the afternoon traffic letting her mind wander as she became one with the bike. She had often wished she had her bike in Iraq but realized that a woman on a motorcycle would have been unacceptable in a country that didn't even let women drive. Besides, all that sand would have fouled up the injection system. She glided to a stop at the light, touching down one foot to the pavement. Looking to her left, she saw a convertible roll to a stop beside her. The driver was the petite blonde, Theresa, from the gym, who was waving and looking at Nic. The stereo was playing a loud rap beat that practically drowned out the rumble of the motorcycle. Glancing at the light and then back to the car, she grinned as Theresa blew her a kiss. Blushing, she turned back toward the light. *What the—* from the corner of her eye she saw the driver give Nic a wink and pucker her lips, simulating a kiss. Shaking her head, Nic chuckled but didn't look over. The last thing she wanted now was an open flirtation on base that could get her a court-martial. The woman honked her horn and motioned for her to pull over. Shaking her head in the negative, Nic just smiled and waited for the light to turn green. Just as it did the blonde hit the gas and sped ahead of her, cut into her lane, and slowed down, forcing Nic to slam on her brakes.

There were a lot of things Nic could tolerate but screwing with her while she was on her bike was not one of them. She drew alongside the convertible and pointed toward an empty parking lot. The young woman pulled over. Her smile was full of eager invitation as Nic approached. "What the fuck do you think you're doing?" Nic growled as she tore off her helmet. "You could have gotten me killed back there."

"Oh, come on. Aren't you being just a little overdramatic?" Hard nipples caught Nic's attention first. The woman's blouse was so shear Nic could see she wasn't wearing a bra. *Her silver nipple rings contrast nicely against her dark areolas,* Nic thought as she stared at the woman's chest. Nic found herself more than a little excited by the sight.

Doing her best to ignore the distracting sight, Nic said, "Look this isn't a game. Someone could have gotten hurt and that someone could have been me. Then what?"

"Come on, no one got hurt." Extending her hand, she said, "By the way, my name is Theresa. And yours is?"

"Trust me, you don't want to know my name," Nic said, towering over the petite blonde. "Now if you will excuse me, I have business to attend to."

"Wait." Theresa grabbed Nic's arm. "I just wanted to get to know you. Is there anything wrong with that? Besides, maybe we could have coffee or something."

"I don't drink coffee, and I'm not your type."

"I know how to handle women like you gorgeous. Trust *me*," Theresa said, her voice husky as she eyed Nic's chest. She ran her hand brazenly over one of Nic's breasts, smiling when she felt Nic's nipple harden.

The simple touch, combined with the adrenalin that whipped through her when the woman cut her off, sent Nic over the edge. She groaned and grabbed Theresa's hand, pinning it to her breast. Somewhere in the recesses of her mind she knew she should stop, but it had been far too long since a beautiful woman had touched her.

"Careful what you wish for," Nic said. She grabbed the presumptuous woman by the wrists, pulling their bodies together. Theresa moaned as Nic tilted her head to the left and pulled her hair, forcing her head back and exposing Theresa's neck to Nic's lips. Nic attacked her neck, kissing it roughly. Nic could feel her pulse speed up. She made her way up Theresa's neck to her jaw, nipping at the perfect little line. Nic continued on to her lips, which were open and begging to be kissed. Crushing the waiting lips underneath hers, Nic slid her tongue inside and heard the woman moan. She caressed the breast beneath the thin blouse, squeezing and pinching the pierced nipple until she could feel the woman grinding against her.

God, what am I doing? She suddenly released the woman, who stumbled back against her car. Nic mumbled an apology, as she turned and got back on her bike. She started her bike, slapped on her helmet and drove out of the parking lot cursing her rash judgment. She could hear the woman shouting something, but ignored it as she sped up.

God, what had she just done? Anyone driving past could have seen them, could have seen her. Nic was on fire, every nerve in her body was exploding and she thought she would come right there on her bike, the vibration adding more stimulation to an already sensitive clit. *Fuck, Fuck, Fuck,* she had to get home and quick. If she was going to have a melt down she didn't want it to be out in public.

It had been months since Nic had even thought about sex. No, that wasn't quite true. Every time she thought about it, she either went to the gym and worked herself to exhaustion or worked late to keep herself occupied. Nic continued to navigate her way back to her place, edgy, frustrated, and definitely explosive. She pivoted her hips on the rolling vibrator, finding a place that not only kept her stimulated, but damn near brought her to climax. Her entire focus was centered on the throbbing between her legs. She turned the bike around at the next light and headed out to a deserted stretch of road. Opening up the throttle, she leaned into the bike allowing her body to feel the vibration of the huge machine as she shifted through the gears. She rocked forward, the seam of her jeans making perfect contact with her clit. Her nipples hardened as she felt the wind rub her shirt roughly against them. Every muscle tensed in anticipation of the impending release, and she could feel sweat breaking out everywhere on her body. She felt herself start to spasm as she rode both the motorcycle and the climax. Nic's hips bucked once, twice, and then a third and final time as she climaxed. It took every ounce of control she had to stay upright on the motorcycle as she pulled to the side of the road.

Nic leaned over, gasping for breath and holding on to the gas tank for stability. Dropping the kickstand, she swung her leg over and flopped to the ground on her hands and knees. *God, what have I just done?* This person was foreign to Nic. She was always in control of her emotions and she never, ever lost control. Sitting back on her heels, taking a deep breath, she could still feel her throbbing clit rubbing against now soaked jeans. She stood, grabbing her jeans at the knees and forcing them down just enough to prevent further contact with her clit. Still hunched over, she worked to control her breathing and her emotions. It had been so long since she had been with anyone that she had forgotten what that felt like. Enough. *No good can come from thinking like this.* No one would want an emotionally bankrupt, broken down soldier. It wasn't worth thinking about.

CHAPTER THREE

When she finally arrived back at her place, Nic stripped off her soaked clothing and headed to the shower for the third time that day. She was spent, but she felt surprisingly relaxed at the same time. It had been a long time since she had felt like this, a long time since she felt normal. What was normal to her now? Nic felt somewhat normal when she was in uniform. She felt normal riding her motorcycle. She felt normal being alone.

In fact, since she had been home from the hospital Nic rarely thought about her love life. To be intimate with someone meant being naked, and that meant there would be questions. Nic wasn't sure she was ready for the type of intimacy that bared her soul to a stranger. It was just easier to wish for a love life than to actually take the steps towards having one. That probably attributed to her lack of a sex drive, but today was different and she didn't know why. Nic definitely wasn't one for casual encounters. They left her feeling empty inside, and as much as her body had wanted her to, it was clearly why she didn't take the woman up on her brazen offer. Well, that and the possibility of being caught having sex in public with a woman on base.

Ever since the accident she felt empty all the time, like there was a void that couldn't be filled. It had hurt so deep it felt like her soul was broken, like her whole reason for living had changed and she didn't know what it had changed to. It wasn't that she didn't have plenty of opportunities for sex. She was constantly being hit on by both men and women in and out of the Corps. Everyone loves a chick in uniform. Right now though, the thought of being intimate with a woman was foreign to Nic. In fact, the military's "Don't ask, Don't tell" policy made it easy to fend of the advances of the other women in the Corps. No officer wanted to lose his or her commission because of that policy, and while Nic didn't agree with it, she had to live with it.

She stepped into the hot shower and the stream of water on her back felt like little needles on her scar. The broken hip had taken no time to heal, probably because she was in such great shape when the crash happened. The doctor had said that because she worked out with weights and had trained in the martial arts Nic had survived what had killed her crew. Being used to taking a pounding and being able to roll with the crash had helped her survive. *Lucky me*, she thought as she remembered hearing the news as she lay in recovery after her hip surgery. *I am no more deserving to live than my crew was, so why me?* Her shrink called it survivor's guilt. *Whatever.* Giving it a name didn't make it any easier to deal with.

Nic got out of the shower and draped the towel around her hips; and wiped the steam from the mirror. This time Nic noticed the lines around her eyes and a few gray hairs in her dark brown shoulder length mane. *Maybe I should really cut it off, and then I wouldn't have to worry about regulations for a few months.* Nic wasn't one to worry about what people thought and she rarely cared what her hair looked like as long as it was clean, neat and squared away. She was tired of pinning it up and it pulled sometimes under her hat when she was in uniform *Yea, maybe a haircut is in order,* Nic thought as she blow-dried the wet strands off her face.

She reapplied a protective bandage on her scar and finished getting dressed, this time in a pair of loose sweats and t-shirt. Realizing she was starving, Nic went into the kitchen to make something to eat. She couldn't cook worth a damn, but she wouldn't starve. Taking the plastic off a "gourmet meal", she saw the blinking light on her answering machine. Throwing the meal into the microwave, she pressed play on the machine.

"Major, this is Sergeant Ross. We have a bit of a problem with Capt. Monroe's remains. Could you please give me a call ASAP? Thank you ma'am."

"Shit, what does he mean a *problem?*" she asked the microwave as she watched the timer count down. Nic dialed Sergeant Ross.

"Sergeant, you had better have good news for me since you left that message."

"I'm afraid not, Major Caldwell. It seems that there is a problem with Capt. Monroe's remains."

"What problem?"

"Well, it appears they've lost him. I have been calling all over Germany and no one seems to be able to tell me where he is. No one."

"Christ, this is a disaster. I will be right down. You haven't called his wife yet, have you?" asked Nic as she tossed her gourmet meal in the trash. So much for dinner.

"No ma'am. I didn't think that was something that should come from me, ma'am. Besides, the Chaplain said you would be handling anything with Mrs. Monroe."

"Did he now? Give me about half an hour to get to the office. And Sergeant, if Mrs. Monroe calls, not that I think she will, but if she does, don't say anything about this. Understand?"

"Yes ma'am."

"See you in thirty," she said as she dropped the phone into the cradle and made her way to the bedroom.

Holy shit, what the fuck happened? What am I going to tell Mrs. Monroe? She's been through so much already. This is just going to send her over the edge. Christ! She couldn't believe that the military could lose the remains of a service member when they had managed to ship over four thousand bodies home successfully.

Thirty minutes later, Nic could feel the tension when she entered the small office. "Sergeant, what have you got for me, and don't say "nothing" if you know what is good for you."

Nic could see the tension in the Sergeants face as he looked up at her and she already knew what the answer was. "I am sorry, ma'am, but Rheinmein says they never got the body in. They have checked their manifests three times and they swear that the body never arrived."

"Great. Get their Duty officer for the airfield on the phone and let's track this down. Wait—" she wondered if the screw-up started there or back in Iraq. "First, get me the field hospital in Iraq, and then if they say they sent Capt. Monroe's remains, we'll talk to the airfield over there to make sure he even left Iraq."

After about a dozen phone calls, she was no closer to finding Mike than when she started. *Christ, now I have to go to Mrs. Monroe's and inform her of the screw-up. Excellent.* Grabbing her hat Nic stood up to leave.

"Sergeant, if I am not back in an hour you better send the Chaplain for me. He will probably have to deliver last rites, 'cause I'll probably be dead or close to it when I inform Mrs. Monroe of *our* screw-up," Nic said as she prepared herself for the coming explosion that was sure to happen once Mrs. Monroe got the bad news.

###

Nic pulled up to Capt. Monroe's quarters and noticed that there were several cars in the driveway and on the street. *Great, now I have to do this with an audience.* Nic knocked and as she had done before stepped down off the stoop and onto the sidewalk. Debbie Rouch, the neighbor who had come over the day before, answered the door, and this time it was clear she too had been crying.

"Major, please won't you come in? A few of the wives have come by to offer their condolences and support to Claire." Walking into the quarters Debbie turned towards Nic and continued, "Can I get you something to drink, perhaps coffee or a soda?"

"No thank you. Would it be possible to speak to Mrs. Monroe?" asked Nic as she advanced further into the house. She peered around the corner of the hallway and saw Claire sitting on the sofa surrounded by a few other wives. Claire had her daughter on her lap as she listened to the conversation swirling around her. Nic noticed her vacant look and was sure that Claire had mentally checked-out of the conversation. Clearing her throat, Nic entered the room full of women, not sure if she should ask everyone to leave or ask to speak to Claire alone. *Well the sooner we get this over with the sooner I can get out of here,* she thought as she slowly made eye contact with each of the women before settling on Claire. The look on Claire's face broke Nic's heart and knowing she was going to add more grief only made her feel worse.

"Mrs. Monroe, would it be possible to speak with you in private?" Nic asked softly.

"Major, is there something wrong?" Claire asked as she hugged her child closer. When Nic inclined her head but didn't say anything, Claire told the group that she was going to put the child down for the night and rejoin them after speaking to Nic.

"Please Major, if you will follow me we can talk while I put my daughter down for the night," Claire said as she walked down the hall to her daughter's room. When Nic entered the room, she was surprised to see model helicopters hanging from the ceiling. On the child's bookshelves, small toy models of helicopters were interspersed with stuffed animals and dolls. There were family pictures of Grace with her parents in what one could only describe as the "perfect family".

Nic watched as Claire focused on getting her daughter ready for bed. She thought about how Mike would never be part of this process again. She suddenly thought about how much she wanted a family like Mike's, a beautiful wife and child to come home to and how that all seemed so foreign to her since the accident. She watched as Claire dimmed the lights and took her daughter in her arms, settling into the rocker in the corner of the room. Crooning softly, Claire rocked back and forth, gently holding Grace. Nic felt like an interloper that had no business seeing such an intimate moment between mother and child and slowly made her way to the door. Just as she reached the door, she heard a soft whisper.

"Major, please. She's almost asleep. Just a minute more."

Humming softly Claire got up and placed the sleeping girl on her bed, covered her and gently rubbed her back to comfort her. Nic shifted from one foot to the other, still uncomfortable witnessing something so loving, and so intimate. Claire rose from the bed and quietly walked to the door, and as she did she slid her hand along Nic's arm, moving her out of the room. A tingle slid along the path Claire's hand had just traveled and unsettled the Major at once, Nic ignored the shiver that traveled up her spine as she tried to focus on the reason she was there.

"I thought we could talk in here. It's quiet and I'll be able to hear Grace if she wakes up," Claire said as she settled herself on the edge of the king size bed. "Please sit down, Major. I am sure whatever you have to tell me you can do sitting. Besides, you're going to strain my neck if I constantly have to look up at you," she said, trying to lighten the mood.

Claire wasn't sure why she was trying to make Nic feel more comfortable considering the events of the last two days but it felt right to try. Claire knew Nic, but only in a cursory way, through dinners and military functions that they both had to attend, one out of duty and one out of honor. She took a deep breath and let it out slowly, knowing that if Nic was here this late it could only mean more bad news.

Looking down at her hands Nic said, "Mrs. Monroe..." she faltered and then cleared her throat. "I am sorry but it seems that your husband's remains are missing."

When she didn't get a response, Nic looked up and saw Claire staring at her. Nic waited a minute and then cleared her dry throat again.

"I am so sorry. I have been on the phone calling

all over Iraq and Germany to find out what happened and no one can tell me a thing. I have my sergeant working on it right now but I felt I should let you know so that you can contact your families and give them the news. Without the remains, we can't plan anything for the service and I am sure you have a lot of plans that need to be made. I mean, that is why I am here, to help you with those plans, but I just thought that you should know and...."

Claire was still staring at her, only this time tears were streaming down her face as she began to sob silently. Not knowing what else to do, Nic slid closer to her and put an arm around her shoulder. Claire turned into Nic and buried her face into the major's chest and began to weep heavily. Nic felt Claire grabbing her BDU top so tightly she wondered if Clare would rip it. Wrapping her other arm around Claire, Nic slowly stroked her back in an effort to comfort her.

"Mrs. Monroe, I am so sorry. I don't know what to say. Please know that I will do my best to find Mike and bring him home as soon as possible. Please, please know how sorry I am." She spoke softly to the young widow wrapped in her arms, crying. Nic started to rock back and forth and softly pleaded with Claire to try to relax.

"Major, I'm not sure I can handle this anymore. I have lost my husband and now you tell me you have lost his body. I'm not sure I can take much more without losing it." She wept, still clutching Nic's BDUs tightly.

"I am so sorry. Please know how sorry I am for having to put you through this."

"Major, I know this isn't your fault, I understand that, but god, how could the Corps lose his body? How could they do this to my family and me? Haven't we been through enough already?" Claire asked, her body language suggesting that the question was rhetorical. Nic knew she wouldn't be able to get those answers, at least not tonight. She settled back as Claire wept harder and pressed against her, looking for comfort, the kind that comes from being held by another person. Nic didn't say anything. At this point, everything seemed so trite.

Nic rested her head on Claire's, feeling her body shake as she started to sob uncontrollably again. Nic could smell her perfume and lilac shampoo. It had been a long time since she held someone like this and the sensation wasn't at all an unwelcome one. However, this definitely wasn't in the protocol description when she went to do an inform. *All I'm doing is offering a shoulder for her to cry on,* Nic told herself.

Slowly, Nic felt Claire's breathing start to come under control and she felt Claire back away. She put her hands on Claire's shoulders to try to create some distance between them.

"Are you all right now? Is there anything I can get you?"

"Yes, Major. There are a couple of things you can do for me. First, please stop calling me Mrs. Monroe. That is my mother-in-law. Second, would you mind informing everyone out there that they can go home and I will see them tomorrow. I'm beat and I don't think I can make polite conversation anymore," Claire said as she laid down on the bed, curling up into a semi-fetal position.

"Of course Mrs. Monroe. I mean, Claire. I'll be happy to ask everyone to leave but I am not at liberty to discuss what you and I have talked about. So if you want them to know you will have to tell them, okay?"

"Fine Major," said Claire, curling into a ball in the middle of the huge bed.

"Mrs.—Claire, will you do me a favor?"

"Yes Major."

"If I must call you by your first name, you must do the same. Pease call me Nic."

"Thank you Nic," Claire said quietly, still curled in on herself.

"Of course."

Walking down the hall Nic could hear the wives talking about Claire and how strong she was as she faced this unbelievable loss. Each one acknowledged that they too would be devastated if faced with a similar situation. In the military, it was a daily battle to stay positive with a loved one in a combat zone. When Nic entered the living room all eyes shifted to her, each with a question or a demand for answers. Nic calmly informed the group that Claire had requested that they all go home and get some rest, and told them that Claire wanted to thank them for their support and she would see them in the morning. When the last wife left, Nic leaned against the door and let out a long sigh, glad she wasn't obligated to inform the wives of the most recent development.

She headed for the master bedroom to let Claire know that the wives had left and that she, too, was leaving. She started to open the door and had just barely caught a glimpse of Claire sleeping when she heard a soft cry from the bedroom behind her. Nic looked over her shoulder at Grace's room and wondered if she should wake Claire, but quickly changed her mind when she heard Claire release a soft snore. *Maybe I can rock Grace back to sleep and then leave and no one will be the wiser. Besides, Claire needs to sleep.* Turning, Nic went into Grace's room and found her sitting up in her bed.

"Hey little one. What are you doing up?" Reaching down, she picked up the child. All at once the little girl latched on to her neck and laid her head down on Nic's broad shoulder. *Must be the uniform*, she thought as she slowly rocked the child back and forth. Grace settled down almost immediately, but each time Nic tried to put the little girl down she began to fuss. Spying the rocker, Nic sat down and slowly started to rock Claire's daughter back to sleep.

So, this is what it would feel like to have a kid. Rocking, she started to feel herself nod off when her phone rang.

"Major, are you all right? Should I call the Chaplain and have him come out to meet you?" asked Sergeant Ross.

"Sergeant, I am fine but you just woke up the baby."

"Excuse me, Major?"

"Oh, never mind. I'm fine. Go home and get some rest. We'll start again in the morning. And Sergeant, not a word of this to anyone, understand?"

"Understood Major, but I have no idea what you are talking about, believe me."

"Good. Now go home to your wife, kiss her and be thankful for what you have, soldier."

Nic began the process of rocking the little girl back to sleep again. She looked down to find Grace looking up at her with the bluest eyes she had ever seen.

"Hmm, whose eyes do you have princess? You're a little cutie, aren't you? I bet you are your momma's pride and joy, huh?"

As she kept rocking, she slowly started to nod off herself. She never let go of the little bundle laying there in her arms.

CHAPTER FOUR

When Claire woke-up she realized that Grace had slept the whole night through. *She must have been exhausted. Poor little bugger has no way of letting all of that stress out.* Looking down she noticed that she still wore her clothes from last night. Claire thought about the events from the night before. *How could they lose Mike's body?* She wished it had all been a bad dream but it wasn't. She wouldn't be able to get through everything until they found Mike and right now she needed a friend. She needed to talk to someone and there was only one person she could count on to be there for her. Claire and Jordan had been best friends all through college and she knew all Claire's secrets. Claire had called her when she got the news of Mike's death, and although she hated to burden those she cared about with her own troubles, the loss of Mike's body was more than she could bear alone right now.

She picked up the phone and dialed the number she knew by heart. Claire took a deep breath and tried to relax as much as she could while she waited for Jordan to answer.

"Hello."

"Hey Jordan."

"Claire? What's wrong, honey?" Jordan asked. "Is everything alright?"

Claire hesitated for a moment and then revealed what had happened. Claire began to cry as she explained what little she knew about the military's loss of Mike's body.

"Honey, do you need me to come out right now?"

"No," Claire said, sucking in a stuttered breath, "I don't know how long it will take for them to find Mike, and Nic, I mean Major Caldwell, said she would call as soon as she heard something."

"Nic? Who's Nic, honey?"

"She's the officer assigned to help us with the military process when someone loses a loved one. She's been making sure that everything moves smoothly as we work through Mike's funeral and stuff."

"I see. Well at least the military is helping you with all of this, since it is their fault Mike is missing."

"Look Jor, I need to get off the phone and shower before Grace wakes up. As soon as I find anything out I'll call. Okay?"

Jordan made Claire promise that she would call as soon as Claire found anything out, no matter what time it was.

Setting the phone down Claire buried her face in her hands and wept silently. She had hoped speaking to Jordan would help, but it didn't. How much more would she have to endure? Mike's parents would be devastated when she told them the news. She would wait on that phone call because she knew Mike's mom would start calling congressmen, senators and anyone else who would listen. Mike's mom meant well, but she lacked the patience to wait for things to happen, though this time Claire couldn't blame her. She decided a hot shower could come before that call.

After her shower, Claire studied her reflection in the mirror. She appeared tired and the vacant stare that looked back at her shocked her. She hadn't looked this bad since high school when she had to face who she really was. Her father had put her through hell and she hadn't handled the stress well. Now wasn't the time to think about that again. No, she needed to focus on Grace and taking care of Mike's affairs. Then she would focus on the future.

Walking to Grace's room, she stretched and shook off the last vestiges of sleep before opening the bedroom door. She needed to be ready for a rambunctious three year old who wouldn't understand that her world had just been turned upside down. Claire wasn't ready for the sight before her as she entered her daughter's room. Claire stood in the doorway, transfixed by the site of Nic and Grace together. Her momentary shock at seeing them together faded as she took in the whole scene. She hadn't noticed before, but now that she could look at Nic openly, she found her striking, almost handsome. Her soft brown hair had come loose while she slept and framed her face, softening her features. Claire studied Nic's face and admired her square jaw, thinking that it made her feminine face look strong and intense. Claire continued her assessment and stared at Nic's lips, wondering how soft they were and if they were firm when kissed, or slack and limp, which she hated. Claire's fingers caressed her own lips as she thought about what it would be like to kiss Nic. *God what am I doing?* Claire thought as she took a deep breath to center herself.

"Major, Nic, wake-up," Claire said very softly just in case Nic startled easily. "Time to get up, Major."

There it is again a honeyed voice telling her to wake up. Nic opened her eyes and saw the most beautiful sight before her. Brown eyes and hair, and full, luscious lips that begged to be kissed. Striking features that reminded her of those Greek goddesses she had read about. Nic let her eyes drift shut again, trying to go back to sleep and dream about her goddess. But the silken request for her to wake up came yet again, only this time Nic felt a hand on her shoulder shaking her awake. *Please go away and leave me to my dreams.*

"Major, it's 6:00 am and I'm sure you need to get ready for work," said the honeyed voice.

Nic felt her back protest at the position she had been sitting in all night. She realized that she wasn't dreaming and she wasn't lying in her bed at home. Nic opened her eyes, and looked directly into Claire's bemused stare as she started to take her daughter out of Nic's lap.

"Oh, ah, sorry Claire. I can explain…" Nic said when Claire raised an eyebrow in question. "I was starting to leave after I checked on you last night, but I heard Grace starting to wake up, so I, uh, just came in here and picked her up. I guess we both fell asleep." She decided to wait until Claire said something before embarrassing herself more.

"Nic, it's ok. I appreciate you looking after Grace and me. But you don't have to feel responsible for us. I'm a big girl and can take care of us, trust me." Claire was trying to take Grace, but her daughter had other ideas as she clung to Nic's neck.

Noticing the look on Claire's face as her child cuddled into Nic's chest, she said, "It must be the uniform." Nic watched as Claire just nodded and smiled. The officer noticed that Claire had showered and changed into a college t-shirt and sweat pants. She couldn't help but notice how cute Claire looked in the oversized clothing. She also noticed Claire hadn't thought to put on a bra and it was obvious. *God, how could I look at her that way?* Nic thought, chastising herself for looking at the widow in an unprofessional manner.

Claire noticed that something had suddenly made Nic uncomfortable as her body stiffened. *Must be how Grace has taken to her,* she thought, reaching for her daughter. Grace gave a weak protest, but as soon as Claire asked Grace if she was hungry, she latched onto her mother and nodded.

"Nic, I am going to make Grace some breakfast. Would you like to join us?" Claire asked, wondering why Nic was staring at the floor rather than at her.

"Thank you for the offer, but I should be getting to the office to find out if there is any news about Mike."

"You're welcome to stay Nic. It's the least I can do for staying with Grace all night. I'm sure that wasn't the most comfortable place you've had to sleep lately."

"It's fine, really. Perhaps a rain check? I really do need to get to the office and see what I can find out."

"I understand Major, but would you mind coming by later? I'm not sure where to start to settle Mike's affairs. Maybe you can brief me as to what the military will need from me and what the time line is for things here."

"Of course. How about if I stop by after lunch? That way I can go home and get a shower and then get a briefing on what's going on at the office. Hopefully, I'll have good news for you. I'll also bring any paperwork that will help in the process and may need your signature."

"That'll be fine, Major."

"Please, remember you promised to call me Nic."

"I'm sorry. Old habits die hard. I'll try to remember."

"Thank you," Nic said as she went outside. Ducking her head towards Grace she grabbed the child's hand and scrunched her nose. "And good-bye to you, too, princess."

Feeling the heat rise in her cheeks, she turned and walked towards her car. Nic didn't know where all of that mushiness came from and was surprised by her own behavior with the little girl. She smiled as she remembered rocking the little girl to sleep the night before. What she wouldn't do for a family of her own. Nic thought about how different her life would be if she had someone to come home to and to share her days and her nights with. Would she give up everything and settle down if she found the right person? In her current line of work, another woman was damn near impossible to find, and with the military's Don't Ask, Don't Tell policy she would never find her as long as she was in the Corps. Well someday, when she had time and was ready to settle down, that was exactly what she would do. Now she just needed the perfect woman. She scoffed at the thought and headed to the office.

As the Major made her way to her office she noticed the clouds that had threatened rain the day before were gone and replaced with a warm, gentle breeze. Nic liked days like this. They reminded her of another time when she didn't have a care in the world and could just sit back and enjoy what nature had to offer. She often spent time outdoors, hiking or hanging out at the beach. She truly loved the beach. It centered her, especially after the accident, when so much of her life had changed. She still found joy in walking along the sand, or sitting and just watching the tides roll in.

Pulling into her parking space at the barracks, the Major noticed that the sergeant was already there. Nic appreciated Sergeant Ross's dedication and reminded herself to tell him that when she got a chance. But right now she needed to help Mike's family get closure. She looked down at her uniform to make sure it wasn't too wrinkled, that her buttons were closed and her boots were laced. Nic always wanted to lead by example. It was her style, and she didn't ask her people to do something she wasn't willing to or hadn't done herself. If you wanted respect you had to earn it and show the people you lead that you respected them too. So far it had worked for her, but there was always that one asshole that had to have his clock reset every once in a while, and Nic wasn't against resetting one every now and then. In fact, she relished having to establish the pecking order occasionally, as it kept everything in perspective.

Nic opened the door to the office and Sergeant Ross stood quickly to attention and called out, "Officer on deck."

It had been an ongoing joke between the two, with Nic admonishing him the first time he had done it. Sergeant Ross had done a tour on a ship, where the custom was to call out the greeting when an officer entered the room.

Nic looked around and noticed that no one had gotten to the office yet, probably because it was the weekend and duty hours were a little more relaxed. Giving him her best evil eye, Nic yanked her cap off and tossed it on her desk.

"Knock it off Sergeant. How many times do I have to tell you that isn't funny anymore? It makes me damn uncomfortable. Save it for the brass asses that come through that door. Next time I am going to drop you for 100 push-ups on my count, got it?" Nic chided the sergeant as she walked passed his desk. She knew how much he hated working out and only did it because it was required, and the three times a week he did bother were barely keeping his gut in check.

"Yes ma'am," he said, saluting as she walked by, knowing that would piss her off just as much. They had a relationship based on mutual respect, and she knew she wouldn't be half as good at her job without Sergeant. Ross, so she tolerated his jokes.

"Any news on the Capt. Monroe's whereabouts?"

"Not yet Major. I have called Germany again and they still don't know anything."

"Great, just great. Well let's call Iraq again and see if they found something."

"Yes ma'am. By the way, I didn't call the Chaplain like you told me to. I figured you were just kidding about the Captain's wife killing you. Besides, I've seen her. You can take her anytime. She's just a little thing," he said, chuckling.

"Looks can be deceiving Sergeant. Remember that Private who nearly cleaned your clock in P.T.? She was little and put you on your ass in about three seconds flat."

"Yeah, I remember. Thanks for the walk down memory lane Major. Can I get back to work now?"

"Hey, far be it from me to stop you from doing your job, Sergeant. By the way do you ever see that Private?" Nic said, chuckling at the blush that had crawled up the Sergeant's neck to his ears.

"Never."

Nic knew Sergeant Ross saw the young Private, who was now a Private First Class, damn near everyday in the mess hall. She still gave him that nod that meant she had him and he knew it.

"Good, I would hate to think that you see her

everyday and she rubs your nose in it. I mean, that would suck royally," Nic said as she passed by Sergeant Ross on her way to her office. Looking down at the papers stacked on her desk, Nic remembered that she had duties other than just doing her informs and she needed to get busy on those as well before her superiors came down on her.

Two hours later, Nic had made a sizeable dent in the paperwork on her desk and her back ached from sitting still too long. Her scar ached as she stood up and stretched her back. Looking at the clock on the wall, Nic remembered that she needed to eat and shower and not necessarily in that order, considering she had slept in her BDU's all night. She grabbed her cap and informed Sergeant Ross that she was going home to shower and change and get something to eat. She looked back at the sergeant when he didn't answer and saw the puzzled look on his face.

"Don't ask. Call me if you hear anything."

"Yes ma'am."

She stopped him as he started to stand up and salute. "Don't even think about it Sergeant Smart Ass or you can drop right now and give me fifty," Nic said, grinning as she walked out the door.

CHAPTER FIVE

Claire sat on her couch, absently twisting her wedding ring. She was thinking about all the things she needed to do to put Mike's affairs in order. Nic had told her she would help, but Claire didn't want to be a burden on anyone, especially Nic. Claire smiled as she thought about finding Nic sleeping with Grace. She should have been concerned when she saw the two together, but she wasn't. Nic seemed so comfortable with Grace and her daughter seemed to be taken with Nic. Claire wondered what kind of woman joined the Marine Corps and then chose to fly helicopters. Someone with something to prove, she thought. Claire knew little about the women of the Corps since Mike was in an attack unit. Women weren't allowed in the combat units and that included an attack helicopter unit. Her access to Marine women was limited to the occasional encounter at a military ball or battalion function.

The more Claire thought about it, the more she wondered if she could have been a rough and tough Marine. Nic had a certain confidence about her that Claire found sexy. *Did I just say sexy and Nic in the same sentence?* She cocked her head to the side, considering the question. It was true. Nic had self-confidence, a bearing that made her stand out from the rest of the Marine Corps officers. She walked with her head high, but lacked the swagger that some pilots seemed to have. Once, Claire had made the mistake of calling one of Mike's friends a pilot. He stopped dead in his tracks, turned and looked her right in the eyes. Without blinking he told her to never refer to him as a pilot— he was a Marine Aviator. Big difference, he said.

No, Claire couldn't see Nic acting like that, pompous and arrogant. Nic had shown her tenderness when she had held her the night before, something she couldn't see a male Corps member providing. Claire remembered how solid Nic felt as she held her while she cried. The smell of Nic's perfume, a subtle mix of clean and citrus had enveloped her while she leaned against the officer's chest. Claire closed her eyes again as she thought about Nic's arms wrapped around her, rocking her back and forth. It almost seemed surreal now, being held by a woman again. The softness of her touch and the gentleness of her voice still rang in Claire's ears. She felt her body start to react at the thought of Nic holding her. She was just the kind of woman Claire had been attracted to in college.

Nic sat in her car, thinking about Claire and everything she was going through. She thought about all of the spouses and families that had to endure the process of burying their loved ones. Then she thought about her own crew and what their families had gone through. Nic had missed all of the funerals and memorials for the crew, her crew. She was in a hospital bed barely able to sit-up, let alone talk to anyone about what happened. Maybe that was why she was taking what happened to Mike so hard, because she knew him, went to college with him, and was stationed at the same base in Iraq. She had socialized with his family at unit functions so it was painful to see what Claire was going through all by herself. Well, soon it would be over for Claire and she would move on to a new life and learn to deal with the loss. Given enough time, they all moved on eventually, and Nic would too. Eventually.

She couldn't get Claire out of her mind. She was a beautiful, vibrant woman who had her whole life ahead of her. After a long, hot shower, Nic opted for a pair of jeans, t-shirt and boots. Now, she felt a little more normal, and more—human. Although it might be strange to people outside the military, as long as she had the uniform on she felt like she should act accordingly. Which in and of itself wasn't a bad thing, but it sure was nice to look like an average civilian occasionally. It was such a beautiful day she decided to ride her bike to Claire's house. The fresh air and freedom would do her soul some good right now. She tucked the necessary paperwork in her saddlebag, wishing she could leave it behind.

Nic leaned over the bike and remembered the last time she was on it. She flushed at the memory and felt a resultant tug between her legs. Nic started the bike, adjusted her helmet, zipped up her jacket and slipped on her gloves. She loved how the bike felt like a part of her every time she rode it. Gliding down the street she didn't think about anything but the machine and the feeling of power and freedom it gave her. And, of course, the occasional car that always seemed to cut her off when she rode.

She decided to take the long way to Claire's house. First, she wanted a longer ride to blow the cobwebs out and reenergize and second, she was confused by the flutter of nervousness in her stomach when she thought of spending more time with Claire. She parked in Claire's driveway and took her cell phone out of the inside pocket of her jacket. She briefly talked to Sergeant Ross who had nothing new to report and promised to call her if anything came up. She informed him that if she was needed, she would be at Claire's for a bit to see if she needed anything before returning to the office to finish up her paperwork.

Just as she was about to knock, the door opened and several women started down the steps. Quickly stepping aside, she avoided running into them, although they weren't paying attention to anyone as Claire said goodbye to them and thanked them for their kindness.

"Oh, sorry, we didn't see you there. Major Caldwell? Is that you? I didn't recognize you out of uniform. Sorry," the woman in front said, this time looking Nic up and down as if inspecting a side of beef.

"No problem ma'am. I'm just here to check on Mrs. Monroe and then I'm off to the office," the major said, slightly irritated that she felt the need to explain her appearance. Turning, Nic caught sight of Claire looking down at her as Claire waved good-bye to the wives.

"Please come in, Nic."

"Thanks. I hope this is a good time for me to come by? I didn't think to call first. Sorry." Nic swallowed hard, wondering what it was about Claire that caused her to lose her train of thought and babble like some school girl. She turned when she heard Grace behind her and quickly lifted the little girl into the air.

"Oh, sorry. I hope it's all right that I picked her up, I just —" Nic said, suddenly aware of what she had done. "She's just so cute and sweet…"

"She seems to be really attached to you, too. You're all she has talked about all day. She told everyone that you spent the night and slept with her in her room. Try explaining that to the wives that just left. Besides, she seems to really calm down when you're here."

"I'm sorry if it caused any problems for you."

"No, not at all. Besides, the other wives are happy that the military is helping out so much."

"Well that's why I'm here. You know, to check on you and Grace and see if there is anything I can do to help out," she said, as she followed Claire into the living room. Nic sat down on the couch with Grace still in her arms. The little girl curled up on Nic's chest and started to doze off.

"Well, if you can come over about this time everyday and do that," Claire said, pointing to the little girl now sleeping on Nic's chest. "It would help out a great deal. She's had a hard time going down for a nap ever since we got the news of Mike's death. I'm sure she's picking up on the stress in the house and doesn't have a way to process it like you and I do. So she's fighting her normal routine."

"Well, I'm not sure I can come by everyday at this time, but I can make it a point to stop by everyday and check in on you two if you would like?"

"Thank you for the offer Nic, but I am sure you have lots of other work that you should be giving your attention to. Besides, I'm a big girl and can take care of myself."

"I'm sure you are Claire. Maybe I can take care of Grace if you would like to do some shopping or just have some time to yourself. I know how stressful all of this can be, really."

Claire heard a catch in Nic's voice and wondered what it meant. Surely, she didn't lose her husband in Iraq, too. She hadn't heard that Nic was married, but that didn't mean anything. She didn't know the personal lives of most of the soldiers in Mike's unit, and unless she knew their wives, she was pretty much out of the loop entirely. Although she had heard rumors about Nic, she didn't give much credence to gossip from the wives. *As if I could be that lucky,* she thought.

"Tell you what. Why don't we put Grace down and I'll fix you something to eat. That is, if you're hungry?" Claire motioned for Nic to follow her to Grace's room.

Closing the door as they left Grace sleeping soundly, she whispered to Nic, "So Major, can I interest you in something to eat?"

Nic swallowed hard, her knee jerk reaction a desire to tell Claire exactly what she'd like to eat, but then her own stomach betrayed her with its noisy rumbling and they both laughed.

"Well, that's settled. Your stomach has answered my question. What can I get you to drink?" She headed for the kitchen and motioned in the direction of the couch. "Sit. So what'll it be?"

After settling on a diet soda, Nic tried to relax on the couch. Looking around, she noticed the photos scattered around the front room walls and bookshelves. Some were of Grace, some of Claire and a few of the family together doing what families often do, picnicking, holidays and the usual stuff. She also noticed Mike and Claire's degrees on the wall along with Mike's Commissioning Papers and his Diploma from Flight school with his first pair of wings. She had the same things tucked away somewhere in a closet rather than on display. She walked over to the pictures and scanned them, focusing more on the pictures of Claire. She heard Claire clear her throat behind her and realized that she was probably out of line.

"Sorry. I was just looking at your family photos.

You look like a happy family."

"Looks can be deceiving," Claire murmured as she handed Nic a plate with an assortment of food on it.

"I'm sorry, I didn't hear you."

"It's nothing. Can I get you something else?" Claire turned and walked back into the kitchen, and Nic noticed the somber look on her face. Deciding to follow her, Nic nearly crashed into Claire, who had suddenly turned around as though to ask Nic something.

"OH! Sorry, I —Can I get you something else?"

"I'm sorry, I was just.... Well I just thought something was wrong and I, well I— Sorry," she said, turning and sitting down at the dining table.

"Look, why don't we sit on the couch? Grace will be up soon and we won't even have had time to eat if we don't sit down now. I guess I'm just tired and haven't had a lot of time to process everything that has happened. Please, let's eat. I'm sure you're starving. Besides, I have enough food to feed the entire unit and it will go bad before we even get a chance to try everything."

"Thank you," Nic said, leaning down and smelling the assortment of foods. "I am kinda hungry. Thanks."

Claire looked at Nic and it dawned on her why she looked so different. Nic's civilian clothes hugged her body and suited her well. She looked comfortable and relaxed. Her tight t-shirt made her broad shoulders and well-defined chest look amazing, and her jeans sat right at her hips, just tight enough to accent her long legs. She noticed Nic's black motorcycle jacket lying across the arm of the couch with her gloves resting on top and realized that Nic had ridden her motorcycle over.

"I don't think I have ever seen you in civilian clothes before. You haven't ever attended the unit or company picnics, have you?"

"No, I usually volunteer to be the OD, officer of the day, so that the officers with families can go and spend time with them. I figure since I don't have a family it's easier for me to do it.

Claire watched Nic eat and wondered why someone so thoughtful didn't have someone special in her life. She knew it was hard for many soldiers in the military to find someone who was interested in them and not just interested in the guaranteed paycheck that the military offered. A lot of women liked the idea of being married to officers, especially pilots. There was a certain amount of prestige that went along with being a flight officer's wife and she knew it. For her it was different—she could care less that Mike was a pilot. It wasn't the reason she married him, but that didn't matter now that Mike was gone.

Without thinking, she blurted out, "So Nic, how come someone as caring as you isn't with someone?" She flushed in mortification. She couldn't believe she had spoken without engaging her brain.

"I'm sorry. You don't have to answer that- it isn't any of my business really." Looking down at her food to hide the rising heat infusing her face, she cleared her throat and began to eat. She couldn't even taste the food as she tried to busy herself moving it around on her plate. Hearing Nic clear her throat she looked up to find a set of cool, green eyes looking at her without any emotion. *Great, now I've done it. I've pissed her off and she's thinking of a way to tell me so.* Looking back down at her plate she speared a few vegetables.

"I'm sorry. I was way out of line Nic."

"No, its fine Claire. It's just that I don't usually have someone asking me about my personal life. I'm usually the one doing the asking." Looking back down at her food Nic debated how to answer the direct question. Should she take the honesty approach or should she deflect and try to answer in a roundabout way without giving up too much information? She thought about it for a while and decided that she would give just enough information to pacify any further curiosity.

"Well," Nic said, "I don't have to tell you how hard it is to find someone who likes this type of lifestyle." Which was true— not too many women wanted to be with someone who was going to be gone for a year or longer and possibly even sent to a war zone. The separation and worry were enough to drive many military spouses to divorce. While many soldiers weren't divorced before they left, many were on the brink when they got home.

"And to be honest I was in a relationship before I was sent overseas. But being sent to a war zone for a year took its toll and we broke up." She stated simply, as though she was just giving Claire a recipe for muffins.

Claire recognized the pain in the flat answer. She had seen the distancing many soldiers or wives formed when they had experienced something so painful that reliving it would open old wounds, and weaken their already fragile existence. She was sure she would be in the same position eventually when someone asked her about Mike. She would be polite, smile, and accept their condolences, but they would never really understand. She watched as Nic pushed her food around on her plate. It was clear she was uncomfortable with the question and now Claire wished she hadn't asked.

"I'm sorry Nic. It's really none of my business. Please eat and let's forget that I said anything." She could see that she and Nic did have some things in common. She just hadn't realized that the loss of a loved one was one of them. In her case, Mike was never coming home. She wouldn't have to worry about seeing him with someone, or imagining him in someone else's arms. Not that she would have worried about that with Mike anyway. Their relationship wasn't like most military relationships, but Nic's pain would hurt in a different way. She would have to think about her ex in ways Claire never would. She had to live with the fact that someone she cared about had chosen a "normal" life rather than stick with her. That kind of hurt was almost worse than what she was going through.

"No, don't worry. It's ok. That isn't really the reason I'm not in a relationship now." Pausing for a moment she wondered why she felt like telling Claire her reasons for not being involved. She hadn't wanted to tell anyone, to open herself up like that and take the risk of appearing weak. Being with Claire felt different for some reason. Losing Mike meant she understood war better than most people, and because of that they had something in common.

"I was wounded in Iraq six months ago and lost my whole flight crew over there. I guess I haven't felt like being back in the swing of things lately because of it." She put another fork full of food in her mouth and began chewing, giving her a reason not to speak. She felt her stomach churn, not because of the food but because she didn't want Claire's pity. She didn't know what she did want, but it sure as hell wasn't her pity.

CHAPTER SIX

The silence quickly became uncomfortable as they both tried to figure out what to say next. Nic felt like she should say something to break the tension that had filled the room and to assure Claire that she was fine and didn't need her pity.

"Wow, I didn't know Nic. I'm so sorry, I—"

"Please, I don't need your pity. I'm fine now." She quickly cut Claire off with a negligent flick of her hand, refusing to look up from her plate. There it was- the start of the pity party starring Nic as the guest of honor. She winced at how harsh her tone was when she heard Claire gasp. *God, why do I have to be so quick to react to someone who's just being nice?* She got up and followed Claire into the kitchen.

Without thinking, she grabbed Claire by the arms and whispered, "I'm sorry. I didn't mean it to come out like that. It's just that... well it's just that I am so tired of people treating me differently when they find out what happened to me."

"Well, you're certainly capable of keeping people from being concerned, aren't you? I mean...." Looking up she saw the hurt in Nic's eyes, causing her to stop in mid-sentence. Her breath caught when she felt Nic's thighs brush her own as Nic held her close. She looked at her feet and instantly regretted her own tone. "I'm sorry, Nic. I was out of line just now. I know you don't need my pity. In fact, I'm sure you're a pretty strong woman because of what you've been through. I just thought that... well I guess I don't know what I thought."

"Please, let's sit down and I can explain. Besides, I'm still a little hungry," she said, hoping to lighten the mood. She let go of Claire's arms and stepped back, trying to quell the butterflies in her stomach and calm her pulse. She liked the way Claire's body felt so close to her own. Close, but not close enough.

Claire refilled the half-eaten plate and put it in the microwave. She turned around and watched Nic take a deep breath and relax a bit as they exchanged glances once again.

Claire didn't know why it mattered what this woman thought, but it did. She didn't want Nic thinking she was a pushy military wife who thought she should be catered to. One who couldn't take care of herself. One who didn't need comfort....

"Can we start over again?" asked Nic as she reached into the microwave before Claire could get there.

"No," said Claire, "why don't we start where we left off? You were going to explain and I was going to keep my big mouth shut."

Nic wanted to argue that Claire had a beautiful, kissable mouth. She wondered where that train of thought kept coming from as she tried to regain her composure. It was clear that she was losing her objectivity when it came to this *inform* and she didn't know why or what was possessing her to take such a personal interest. She took a deep breath and reminded herself to be professional.

Nic walked back to the couch and sat waiting for Claire to join her before she divulged her story. She wondered if it was wise to tell Claire her tale, since it would likely mirror Mike's experience and give Claire a bleak image of Mike's last moments. No, it might not be wise, but she had opened the door, and it felt wrong to push Claire away by not answering her honestly.

Nic spoke so softly that Claire had to lean in to hear the soft words as they came rushing out. "I was flying medivac in Iraq. It was just a routine flight. We had done it a hundred times." She felt herself drifting into the dreamlike state that came when she relived the accident. Her body reacted to the surreal feeling of flying, just like the day of the accident.

"We were returning to the airbase where we dropped off our wounded and pretty much treated it like a routine flight, which was our mistake. We weren't watching for anything out of the ordinary. We were talking about what we were going to be doing when we all returned home in a few months. I remember one of my guys had gotten a letter from home telling him he was going to be a dad again. He was so happy with the news, and was telling us he was hoping for a son this time."

Nic stared into space, every feeling and smell as fresh as it had been the day it happened. Tears rested on her lashes, waiting to be let free. Claire put a hand on her knee, squeezing it gently.

"Anyway, we were starting to bank towards the airfield when it happened. We were hit with a missile round about 200 feet off the deck. The explosion hit the back compartment of the helicopter killing most of my crew and dropping us like a lead balloon. All I remember was hearing a loud explosion, seeing a bright light, and then waking up on the ground with a shooting pain in my back and hips. I smelled something burning around me and then I could feel heat on my back. So I tried to move but I was pinned by the exhaust pipe of the 'copter. I guess when it exploded it threw me and the crew in every direction and blew up the 'copter into a thousand pieces. I realized that the burning smell was my flight suit melting and that if I didn't do something quick I was screwed. I tried standing again but it was no use, so I tried rolling to my side, which is what made my injuries worse. When I rolled, my broken hip punctured through my skin and I started bleeding. However, when I rolled I was able to dislodge the exhaust pipe from on top of me, pretty much taking my flight suit with it and leaving me with second and third degree burns. I don't know how I survived, and no one that looked at the crash site can tell me how I survived. I was the only one that did."

By now Nic was sweating, her t-shirt looking like she had just run ten miles, and she was breathing hard. She was trying to control the tears that threatened to fall but was having no luck. They streamed down her face like tiny tributaries. She always lost control when she recounted the story, and until now, she had never told the story outside her therapist's office for that very reason. Her tight rein on her emotions was slim at best. As long as she compartmentalized the events she was fine. She took a deep breath and tried to control her breathing, fearing she looked like a wild animal. She didn't want to scare Claire and she was afraid that if she looked up she would once again be faced with the look of pity that she hated.

Taking a deep breath she focused on Claire's hand on her knee and finished her story. "I was airlifted to Germany where I was stabilized and then moved to the States for the surgery to repair my badly damaged hip and to treat my burned back. It was a long process and I wasn't able to tell my crew goodbye. The funerals and memorials were done and over with before my surgeries and burn treatments were healed. It took a long time for me to come to terms with what happened over there. To be honest, I'm not sure I ever will, but I'm working on it. The military makes me see a shrink and talk about it and I still have to do rehab, but now I'm down to once a week. I just got released to ride my motorcycle so that helps, too. Now you know why I'm not involved with anyone. Why would anyone want to take on an old war horse like me?" She laughed wryly, hoping she didn't sound as cynical as she felt.

"I can understand what you're going through with Mike because I've been there. It's different, I know, since he was your husband, but I loved the members of my crew like family. I was the pilot. It was my job to get them out of there. I failed them, and I survived." Nic brushed the tears from her face in an angry swipe, irritated that she had let the story get the better of her in front of someone she was supposed to be comforting in the face of her own loss.

Nic watched as Claire moved closer, touching her shoulder.

"Sorry," Claire said quickly when Nic jumped, "is that the shoulder that is injured?"

She was used to the standoffish nature of the shrink's demeanor. It helped keep her focused. Instead, she was staring at Claire's long, perfect hand on her knee and trying to ignore the sudden desire that coursed through her. Claire's closeness was overwhelming and unsettling.

Nic cleared her throat and tried to control her breathing. Claire moved her hand and despite herself, Nic felt a sense of loss at the break in contact. Then Claire softly touched her shoulder instead and Nic jumped like a nervous rabbit.

"Um, actually it's my back. You can probably see the long bandage that I wear to protect the scar." Pointing to her injured left side she shifted so Claire could see her back and then looked over her shoulder, gauging Claire's reaction. Watching Claire's eyes travel her back she shivered slightly and sat up a bit straighter.

"Oh, right, I see it now. I guess I never noticed it before. Does it still hurt?"

"The scar or the hip?"

"Both. I noticed you don't walk with a limp. Was it bad? The hip surgery, I mean."

"Well I guess in the grand scheme of things not too bad. A lot of rehab and hard work is the reason I don't limp. The surgeons said it would be at least six months before I would walk, the injury was so bad, but I couldn't stand being laid up that long, so I worked hard to get on my feet again. I have a total hip replacement in there, ball and socket. So, I should be good to go for about 10 years, if I take care of it and don't abuse it. I can do pretty much anything I did before." Suddenly feeling like a jerk, Nic apologized again. "Look, I am sorry about earlier. I shouldn't have jumped on you like that. You didn't know."

"Nic, please don't apologize again. I see now that you know exactly what I'm going through and I should be the one to apologize. It is none of my business what happened or why you're single. I'm truly sorry. Can you forgive me for being so intrusive?" Suddenly that was the only thing that mattered to Claire. This person not only understood what she was going through but she had been through it herself and survived. She felt like an ass and wanted so desperately to find a way to make it up to Nic.

"Don't give it a second thought. Let's talk about

something else, shall we?"

"Okay, so you were saying that you ride a motorcycle. Can I see it?"

"Sure, it's right out front, but will the baby be ok?" she asked, concerned about leaving Grace alone. She didn't want to seem like she didn't care about the child's safety.

"I'll take the baby monitor with us. That way we can hear her if she wakes up. I'll be right back."

Watching Claire walk away, she was relieved to be off the subject that still caused her so much pain. She chastised herself for her outburst at Claire. *She was being polite and just making conversation,* Nic told herself. Looking up, she saw that Claire had grabbed the walkie-talkie like device that would alert them if Grace woke-up and was heading towards her.

"Ready Major?"

"When you are, ma'am," she said laughing. She chuckled at the exaggerated exuberance Claire was showing as they walked out to view her bike. She wondered if Claire had ever ridden a motorcycle before or if she just liked to look. She walked out and grabbed her keys to the machine so that she could show off its raw power. It was hard to find a woman that wasn't afraid of a motorcycle, let alone to find someone who liked to ride. Any woman Nic was involved with had to at least like to ride behind her, otherwise they were doomed as a couple. A few women Nic dated had said they liked to ride, or at least thought they liked it. However, when push came to shove they were too scared to get on the back. Maybe that was a metaphor for Nic's love life? It was something she had to think about, but not right now. Right now she just wanted to show Claire her ride, her sanctuary, her respite when the world closed in on her.

"Wow Major, nice ride. Have you been riding long?" Claire asked as she looked over the chrome marvel. She was walking around it as if it was an object she had never seen before, remarking on its custom paint job and aftermarket chrome package that Nic spent hours polishing. It was obvious that it was Nic's baby. The attention to detail was amazing and impressive. Claire walked around the bike asking an assortment of questions, surprising Nic.

"So have you ridden before, Claire?" she asked, expecting the pat answer of *No but I would like to some day,* that she always got from women.

"Actually Nic, you could say that." Turning, Claire motioned for Nic to follow her to the garage. Hitting a button and watching the door open Claire turned to watch Nic's reaction when the door was fully raised. Inside stood a fully-dressed cruiser, with a custom paint job, and all the chrome a person could handle polishing.

"Holy shit! Is this Mike's bike?" she asked, running her fingers over the seat.

"Excuse me?" Claire said quietly.

Realizing her mistake by Claire's tone Nic quickly back peddled. "Oh. Sorry, I just assumed that—"

"What, Major? That women don't have their own rides? Or that we only ride bitch, except for those self-anointed few like yourself that are strong minded and self-sufficient enough to ride without a man? No, I ride and Mike didn't." Claire crossed her arms over her chest and glared at her.

Nic definitely knew she had struck a nerve with Claire, and felt its sting in both her words and her body language. She suddenly understood that there was so much she didn't know about Mike and his wife, which wasn't surprising, actually. But when it came to Claire, she was learning she liked surprises. She found herself doing exactly what Claire had just done, walking around Claire's bike in appreciation.

"You're right. I was out of line when I assumed that this was Mike's. In fact, I'm pleasantly surprised to know that this is your ride. So how long have you been riding?"

Letting the question hang in the air, Claire wasn't sure she was quite ready to let Nic off the hook. It pissed her off that people often assumed that Mike was the bike rider in the family when he couldn't stand to ride. She also got mad when people just dismissed it as a phase and told her she should just be an officer's wife and mother and remember Mike's career. She was her own woman and had been when she met Mike. She wasn't the average officer's wife. So she just looked at Nic, thinking she was just like all the other officers who assumed that wives lived for their husbands and their careers. She waited until Nic looked up at her again before she spoke.

"Look Major, I am not the typical officer's wife and I am damn sick of being treated like I live for my husband's career. I've seen it over and over again, wives who have careers and lives outside the military are patronized by those wives who don't. It sickens me. I'm tired of being marginalized by a system and a group of people who don't give a shit about anything but appearances."

Nic was taken aback by Claire's tone and realized she had made a huge mistake. She looked at Claire's angry expression and wondered how she was going to smooth this situation over. She had apologized for her flagrant error when she assumed the motorcycle was

Mike's so she didn't know what to say or do next. So she went with her gut.

"I really am sorry, Claire. You're right. I was way out of line. It's just that I don't meet many women, especially officer's wives, who ride. I mean, I love to ride and I just assumed that I was an anomaly, that's all. Most of the women that I meet who ride are *different*, if you know what I mean."

Just as quickly as her anger had flared, Claire felt it leave. "I'm sorry Nic. You're right. How would you know that I ride? Besides, I'm taking my frustration out on you for the way I've been treated by a few uppity wives." Claire turned towards the motorcycle, trying to hide her embarrassment. Nic was staring at her, making her a bit uncomfortable. It had been a while since anyone had paid any attention to her. She was always Mike's wife or Grace's mom but she was rarely looked at for herself and she realized she was enjoying the attention again. *But is it appropriate to feel this way?* She had just lost her husband, and her child needed a mother more than she needed attention of her own right now.

"So, again, how long have you been riding, Claire?"

"Well, to be honest, I guess you could say I'm a seasoned rider. When my parents divorced, my father thought that it would be fun to teach his kids to ride a motorcycle, and a fun way to spend time with us. So I have been riding since I was about twelve." Claire was proud of the fact that she was a serious rider, with lots of riding experience, and not just a *once in a while* rider.

"It must be hard to ride with Grace and with Mike overseas...." Nic realized her mistake immediately and wished she could take it back. "I'm sorry. I seem to be putting my foot in my mouth a lot today. I'm not normally this careless," she said. "Well, I guess I'm not this careless because I rarely have in depth conversations with many people, especially family members of other Marines."

Hoping to change the conversation back to motorcycles, her favorite topic, Nic asked. "So when was the last time you went for a ride?"

"Well, let me think." Claire put her finger to her temple dramatically, and closed her eyes as if she was in deep contemplation. "That depends on what you call a "ride", Nic. I have a girl who lives down the street who baby-sits for me when I need to run errands and I can't take Grace. For things like Dr.'s appointments, the gym, and stuff like that, I usually take the bike. It gives me a reason to ride since she isn't with me and I can have a little freedom, if you know what I mean. I haven't been on a ride for longer than, say, twenty minutes in so long that lately I take whatever I can get."

Nic could hear the longing in Claire's voice, and saw the wistful look in her eyes as her fingertips played over the chrome handles. Nic was sympathetic to Claire's plight. It had been all she could do to stay sane when she was rehabbing and wasn't able to ride her motorcycle. Sometimes she would daydream about a trip she had taken on her bike, and although it seemed to help with the stress, it also seemed to add to the anxiety when she was frustrated with her progress. The day the doctor had given her the OK to ride again she did just that, coming home and putting on her gear as fast as she could and hopping on her bike. The problem was that while the mind was willing, the body was a different story. She found that she was using muscles that hadn't had a workout in months and she wasn't used to the constant tension and pressure on her shoulders, let alone the pressure on her injured hip. It took her about a month to readjust to the bike and the constant vibration the machine put on her body. After a while she didn't notice the small discomforts caused by riding because of the relaxed state she found herself in after a ride.

"Look, well, I was thinking…." Nic faltered, trying to stop the offer from making it to open air. Claire wasn't a friend. She was a duty.

"Spit it out, Nic. I won't bite, trust me," Claire said with a wide smile that lit up her face and made Nic's stomach flip.

"I was just thinking that maybe we could go for a ride sometime, I mean if you want to, that is. Maybe you could have the babysitter come over and take care of Grace and we could go for a ride, but probably not until after everything has settled down." Realizing how insensitive she sounded she quickly back peddled. "I'm sorry, I shouldn't have suggested that I was out of line. I mean with everything that is going on I'm not being very respectful." *God, how could I be so selfish?* Nic pressed her lips together wishing she could put a lock on them.

Claire only hesitated for a moment. "I would really like that, Nic. I find riding very therapeutic. It helps me process my day and relaxes me and I think I'm a better mother when I get home. So yes, let's do it."

Moving to stand in front of Nic, she took Nic's hand and held it. "And, Nic, you really need to quit apologizing every time you think you've said something wrong. It's all right. I'm not that fragile, honest. Besides, you don't really know about my relationship with Mike. I mean, well, we…." Just then the baby monitor went off with Grace babbling something in her bedroom. "Oh, it's not important," she said, pausing briefly. She suddenly realized she was about to confide in a near stranger about the truth of her relationship with Mike. She opted not to, since she suddenly realized she wouldn't be seeing Nic after Mike's funeral anyway.

"I need to get inside if you don't mind Nic." Making it a statement rather than a question, she walked past Nic and into the house, and as she did, she hit the garage door button.

CHAPTER SEVEN

Nic had decided to take a much needed day off and ride to the ocean. As Nic cruised down the street, she wondered what Claire had been about to say before being interrupted the day before. *It's none of my business how the Monroe's lived,* she thought. Putting it out of her mind she concentrated on her ride. She could smell the clean air, and feel the heat of the day warming her through the leather jacket. It had been awhile since she had taken the bike out on the picturesque drive and she wondered why she had waited so long. *Oh yeah, rehab and informs,* her two least favorite things to do these days. She let the surging traffic take her along the open highway, picking up speed as she maneuvered in and out of traffic.

She watched as the beach opened up on her right-hand side and thought about taking that walk she had planned to make a few days ago. The ocean was cool on the Pacific coast side. In fact, it was downright cold and left her with little desire to swim in it. Nonetheless she loved the west coast a lot more than the placid east coast beaches. The Pacific had that unsettled beauty that often echoed her moods. She had been a rebel in her youth and was often amazed that she had lasted as long as she had in the military.

Her dad often commented that he thought that she would be kicked out the first time someone told her to drop and do push-ups, opting instead to tell them where to stuff those push-ups. But she had surprised him and everyone else, flying through ROTC and Officer Basic, both at the top of her class. She knew why she did it—because someone had said she couldn't and she was just stubborn enough to want to prove them wrong. Being told only men could be good officers and pilots probably had something to do with it, too.

Regardless, she had made it this far, surviving both the military and the war. But now she felt it was time to make some decisions regarding her future. She had known this day was coming and sitting here on the back of her bike gave her some time to mull options over without any distraction. She took the exit to Del Mar and coasted her bike down the winding road. She had to be careful with all of the locals and tourists who loved this part of the world as much as she did. She wound in and out of traffic taking 15th Street to Sea Grove Park, one of her favorite spots in San Diego. A person could look from Dana Point to La Jolla while sitting in the park. It didn't hurt that there was no shortage of beautiful girls to look at either. Nic never objected to eye-candy and San Diego had its fair share of bikini clad bodies year-round.

Nic found a parking space and drifted into it. She pulled her sunglasses off, slid her helmet off her head and shook her hair out as she sat and watched a few kids flying kites down on the beach. She stood and stretched, wondering how long she would be in San Diego. Her recovery was right on schedule. In fact, it was a little ahead of schedule, but she wasn't in a hurry to go back overseas again. She felt bad for thinking that, but she had damn near lost her life and wasn't in a hurry to put it back on the line for a cause she didn't believe in.

Her thoughts drifted to Claire and what she was

going through. She was, without a doubt, one of the stronger wives she had met in the unit. She was handling Mike's death with an inner strength that was admirable. She wasn't like some wives who were so dependant on their husbands to the point of being unable to function without them. She had gone on informs where the wife didn't know where their life insurance policies were, who their finance companies for their automobiles were and some even had husbands that paid all the bills online from overseas. She had met one or two who were definitely the matriarch of the family, but they were rare.

Nic wanted a partner, not a dependant. She wanted someone who would never be above or below her, but always right beside her. She wanted someone who was both independent and someone who wanted to share a life together. She knew that being with someone who was independent could be a blessing and a curse but communication was the key to any relationships survival and she thought she was a pretty good communicator. Okay, she hadn't been doing so well with Claire, but she couldn't figure out why. Every time she was with Claire, she became tongue-tied and babbled like a schoolgirl. *What is it that throws me for a loop when I'm around her?* Sure, she was beautiful, and she had all the things that Nic looked for in a woman. A great body, long brown hair, big brown eyes, soft features, and the most kissable lips she had seen in a long time. The main problem, a big one at that, was that Claire wasn't gay. Certainly not according to Nic's gaydar.

There was no way she would go down that road. She had friends who tried to get with straight women. It always ended up the same–the straight woman was "just trying it out" because she had thought about it once or twice in college or had a friend she had kissed in college and she thought that she *might* be a lesbian. Then after a few weeks or months, she always found out she really wasn't. The few friends it had happened to were devastated from the experience and warned her off about ever trying it for herself. Nope, no matter how beautiful the woman or how horny she was, she would just wait and find someone she connected with.

Nic suddenly realized she hadn't moved the whole time she was thinking about Claire. She looked around to see if anyone noticed that she hadn't moved since getting off her bike. She didn't want anyone thinking she was a weirdo or something. Not seeing anyone looking at her, Nic took her keys from the ignition and strode to the grassy area of the park. A soft breeze ruffled her hair and she turned to the ocean to look out over it. She loved the way the salty scent was stronger depending on the weather. It seemed the sunnier it was, the less salty it seemed. Yet when it was cold and cloudy, it was definitely different, the salt hung in the air with the mist.

She sat on a park bench that fronted the ocean and watched as a few kids were gliding their kites in the soft breeze, just strong enough to put them aloft. She wondered what it would be like to have kids, the responsibility, the love and the time it would take to raise at least two. She never thought that she wouldn't have kids, she just never really thought about who would carry them. Or maybe they would both carry one? However, she definitely saw herself with a couple of kids, a wife, a mini-van and a dog. She hadn't let herself think about it since her accident, but it was time to make some decisions as far as the military was concerned. As long as she was in, she couldn't have those things so she would have to get out if she wanted any of it.

Her time on active duty was almost over, and she had served almost all of her time that she owed ROTC and flight school. She was looking at another six months, maybe a little longer, and then she could go to the inactive reserves or she could find a home in a National Guard unit, if she wanted to. The problem with the National Guard was that they were going overseas as fast, if not faster, than the active Marine Corps and she didn't want to go back overseas. In fact, she wasn't sure she wanted to go into the Reserve Corps either. She had her Bachelor of Science degree in Engineering and knew she could find a job either with the civil service or out in the real world. She had wanted to get her Masters degree, but knew if she did it while in the military there would be more time to serve and she didn't know if she wanted to do that again. She sighed and tossed a pebble out on the sand.

There was just one wild card in all of this, and it was the military. If they put a stop-loss out then no one got out until the military said they could, even if they had done their time, and that would change everything for a lot of people. With her accident and her injuries she might be able to "fly under the radar" so to speak, but she couldn't bank on anything until she saw her orders in her hand, approving her release from service. But she was getting ahead of herself. As far as the military was concerned her future was tied to them and until she served all of her time she was their property, lock, stock, and broken-barrel.

She thought about Claire again as she watched the sun start to dip closer to the horizon. She marveled at how easily Claire slipped into her thoughts. Perhaps she should go by and check in on Claire, *just to make sure she is all right,* she reasoned. Plus, after Grace had woken up the day before, Claire had seemed to shut down, and had pretty much stopped talking. Figuring that she had overstayed her welcome, Nic had left with a promise to herself to do the paperwork another day. Today would be good, as she hadn't seen her, or even spoken to her, and so wouldn't seem over-eager. She could call the sergeant before going over to Claire's so she could give the widow the latest update on Mike. While she knew better than to get involved with a straight woman, she reasoned that there was nothing wrong with spending time with someone she liked and found attractive, even if it wasn't going anywhere. *Right?*

When she pulled up in front of the house, she spotted Claire and Grace standing outside talking to a few women who had their children in tow. The group glanced over in Nic's direction and dispersed. One woman stood by Claire's side, like a sentinel or protector of sorts. A pang of jealousy shot through Nic at the thought, but she just as quickly banished it from her mind. *Remember Claire is straight. Claire is straight.* She realized that being considered a bearer of bad news, and therefore a reason for people to avoid her, bothered her as well.

"Good afternoon, ladies."

"Good afternoon, Major," both women said in unison.

"I happened to be on my way home and thought that I would stop by and check-in to see if there was anything you needed? And to see if you were ready to do that paperwork, Claire."

"Well I should be going, Claire," Mrs. Rouch announced when it was clear that Nic didn't have any more bad news. Claire thanked her and the woman sauntered away, her hips swaying as though she knew she was being watched.

"She wouldn't by chance be Colonel Rouch's wife, would she?" Nic asked, now realizing why the woman rubbed her wrong. It wasn't uncommon for some officer's wives to wear their husband's rank around the younger wives. It was done subtly, but they often threw their weight around by using their husbands rank as a way of getting the things they wanted. Pilots were the elite of the Corps, however, helicopter pilots were thought to be below those that flew jets. None-the-less many of these wives used their husband's rank as a sort of entitlement.

"Why, yes she is. Do you know her?"

"Not really, but I know of her husband. He's over in Iraq right now isn't he?"

"Yes he is. It looks like his tour will be extended there too, but Carol seems okay with it, I guess." Claire said, turning to walk into the house with Grace on her hip.

"Really?"

"Yea, surprising isn't it."

"Not really. She's a bitch," Nic threw her hands up and shrugged when Claire turned to look at her. "So I hear."

"Well, come in and let's get that paperwork started."

CHAPTER EIGHT

Nic followed Claire inside and grinned as Grace smiled at her over her mom's shoulder.

"Hey, cutie. How have you been?" She grabbed the youngster's outstretched hand and shook it. Grace smiled back at Nic giggling as she shyly put her head down on her mothers shoulder, still looking cutely at the woman who was commanding her attention.

Stopping in the entryway, Claire looked back at Nic, her face flushed and her eyes wide. "Excuse me, Nic, what did you say?" she asked.

"What? I... well I was... wait, did you think I was talking to you just now?"

"Well, weren't you?"

"Actually, I was talking to Grace, not that you're not a beautiful woman. Please don't get me wrong, I mean ...." Nic knew she was digging herself deeper but she just stood there, tongue tied, before stumbling in again. "I mean you're beautiful and all but I wouldn't call you 'cutie,' I mean, I would describe you as stunning, and breathtaking ... I mean if I was a guy I would definitely call you those things." She gave a half smile and turned her attentions to Grace, hoping that it would change the subject.

"Isn't that right, cutie?" she said, hoping to reinforce her earlier statement by directing it at Grace once more. "You're the little cutie aren't you?"

Claire stood still as the complements from Nic

rolled around in her brain. It had been a long time since anyone had called her beautiful, stunning or breathtaking and she felt a slight tingle develop in the pit if her stomach. Trying to shake off the sensation, she looked at Grace, who was eating up the attention, too. It had been a long time since anyone had taken an interest in the two of them. Even when Mike was home, he wasn't really *home*. Well, that part of her life was over now and she could start to think about how she really wanted to live her life. At least, she could after Mike's burial.

Turning back toward the living room, she put Grace on the couch and turned toward Nic. She noticed how beautiful her face was when she smiled. It had a softness that surprised Claire, probably because she only saw her when she was in her military persona. But yesterday she had also seen a different side of Nic, one that she never expected to see, either. Both sides were comforting and… she realized she was searching for a word to describe a feeling she hadn't experienced before. Trying to regain her equilibrium, she focused on reality.

"So Nic, is there any news about Mike yet?" she asked.

"No, I'm sorry there isn't. I called my sergeant just before I got here and he said there isn't any news from Germany or Iraq."

"Well, I am a little surprised to see you here then."

"I was on my way home and I thought I would check in to see if you needed anything," she said as she played with Grace and looked at Claire. She had noticed Claire staring at her. Claire's gaze flowing over Nic's body, causing a rush of energy to run through her. She liked being around Claire. It made her feel something she hadn't in a while. She tried to tell herself she was just being protective and supportive, or perhaps she felt sorry for Claire.

"Well, since you're here would you like to stay for dinner? We have plenty of food, remember?" Going into the kitchen, Claire peered around the corner at Nic, hoping she would say yes. "Besides, you would be doing me a favor if you kept Grace company while I made us all something to eat. What do you say? " She asked hoping that Nic would stay and spend time with Grace. *For Grace's sake of course,* she told herself.

"Well, since you put it that way, I can't seem to deny this little cutie anything, can I? Is there anything I can do to help?" asked Nic, as she played with Grace on the living room floor. She found herself crawling on all fours chasing the youngster around the couch as Grace squealed in delight. She stopped behind the couch and waited for Grace to come running around the other side of the furniture, ready to pounce on her the minute she made the corner. She sat there waiting, but instead felt Grace pounce on her from behind abruptly. She jerked in response to having her scar touched and then quickly rolled to her back, pulling the little girl in front of her. She protected her back and took a deep breath to adjust to the sharp pain that had taken her by surprise. At that moment, Claire came around the corner of the kitchen and saw Grace jumping on Nic's back and the brief look of pain that crossed her face.

Nic recovered quickly, but Claire knew that it had to be painful for her to have reacted that way. Quickly Claire scooped Grace up from Nic's grasp and knelt down to see if the Major was all right.

"Nic, are you all right?" she asked, hoping that Grace hadn't done any permanent damage to the healing scar. "I'm so, so sorry." Grace started to cry at suddenly being jerked from Nic's grasp, clearly wondering what she had done wrong. The worried look on Claire's face took Nic by surprise, but not nearly as much as having Grace grabbed from her.

"I'm sorry Claire. Are you mad that I was rough housing with Grace?"

"What, are you crazy? She jumped on your injury and could have made it worse. Why don't you get up and let me look at it. Besides, it was cute the way you two were playing just a minute ago. She hasn't had someone do that with her in a long time." Claire sat down next to Nic and motioned for the other woman to sit up so she could look at the scar.

"Look, I'm fine, really. It was just a little shock to the system that's all. Right Grace?" she said, trying to comfort Grace, who was still crying with her lower lip sticking out. "It's okay really, see," she said, making a silly face.

"No, Nic. I want to check your back, and now. I will not take no for an answer, period."

"If I take the bandage off, it won't be covered and I need to cover it to keep my shirt from sticking to it."

"No problem. I am sure I have plenty of gauze and bandages here to cover your scar. So, just march yourself into that bathroom and get undressed so I can take a look at it. Now!" she said rather sternly to Nic, pointing in the direction of the bathroom. "Go."

Nic just shook her head and acquiesced, figuring it was better than putting up a fight.

CHAPTER NINE

N ic shifted her balance and shuffled her feet, pulling the towel tighter against her chest. She was going to do something she had yet to do with anyone. She was going to let someone actually see her scar. She felt like she was opening her soul to Claire just by letting her see it. Claire sat down on the toilet behind her feeling her anxiety building.

"Ready?"

Nic felt Claire reach up and put her hand on the top of the bandage waiting for her to answer.

"As ready as I'm ever gonna be."

"I'll try and be careful, Nic."

"I know you will."

Nic felt Claire caress her back reassuringly, touching the bandage around its edges. Nic didn't let her guard down easily, but here she was, sitting on Claire's tub, opening herself to Claire and letting her see something so personal. Something no one, besides hospital staff, had been allowed to see.

Nic took in a deep breath. "You might want to go slow when you take off the tape. It's pretty sticky."

"Okay I'm going to start at the top and pull it down slowly. Ready?" Claire said, giving Nic a chance to prepare her mind and body for what was to come. Claire placed one hand on the right side of Nic's back bracing herself to pull the bandage off. She couldn't help but notice the softness of Nic's skin as she placed the palm of her hand on Nic's back. Her fingers wrapped around her slender rib cage, accidentally touching the side of Nic's breast. A surge of heat rushed through her body as she realized where her fingers were.

"Oh, sorry about that," Claire murmured as she moved her hand back towards the center of Nic's back.

Nic felt her body react to Claire's touch. Feeling Claire's fingers graze the side of her breast caused her nipples to harden immediately. *Oh God, I don't know if I can do this,* she thought, as the touch of Claire's hand on her back made her heart beat faster.

"That's okay."

"Ok, here goes." Slowly, Claire pulled down the bandage over the burn. She felt Nic's back tighten as she finally pulled the last of the bandage off the bare back. Looking at the scar, it was clear that she had needed a skin graft to cover the long narrow burn. The edges were red and taunt while the inner portion of the skin graft seem to be fine. Claire gently ran her fingers over the edges of the scar, careful not to touch the actual scar itself. She could feel Nic shiver in response to her touch.

"I'm sorry. Am I hurting you?"

"No, not at all. It's just a little cold in here," Nic lied. Claire's touch was sending chills through her body that she couldn't control. It was all she could do not to lean into the soft hands that were touching her. Feeling Claire's warm breath on her back, she wondered what it would be like to feel her hands on other places, caressing her, touching her, making love to her. *God, what am I thinking. This woman just touches me and suddenly I'm thinking about making love to her. This is not good.* She was still thinking about Claire's touch when she heard her saying something.

"I am sorry. What did you say?"

"Well it looks okay, Nic, but I think maybe you should let it air out a little to help the healing."

"I usually do that at night when I go to bed. I sleep without a shirt on so that it airs out." She turned around so Claire couldn't see the heat rising in her face. The information was too personal, too intimate. She stiffened and half-hoped that Claire would move away from her.

Claire sensed that Nic was embarrassed but she figured it was because she was sitting naked from the waist up in front of someone she barely knew.

"Did it hurt when they did the graft?" Claire couldn't help but stare at the healing injury.

"Not too bad. The place where they took the skin hurt worse."

The burn was almost healed. It wasn't as bad as she had thought it would be. Claire knew that the real injury was the one to Nic's soul and she wondered how long it would take to fix that pain.

Suddenly Grace walked into the bathroom, catching both women by surprise. Claire reached down and scooped up Grace turning her away from Nic.

"Grace, honey, why don't I get you a cookie and you can watch your favorite show on TV." TV was a treat for Grace, and Claire knew it would give her the time she needed to reapply a bandage to Nic's back.

"Okay," said the jubilant child as she jumped down from her mother's arms and raced to the sofa.

"It's okay, Nic. She is used to seeing me naked," Claire said as she wiped her hands off.

The statement made Nic's heart race as she thought about seeing Claire naked.

"Let me get Grace settled and then we can get your back bandaged up. Okay?"

"No problem. I'm not going anywhere."

When Claire left the bathroom, Nic rested her elbows on her knees and ran her hands through her hair. Here she was, sitting in a woman's bathroom that she barely knew, naked from the waist up and daydreaming about Claire touching her. She was starting to feel like she was on emotional overload with Claire seeing her scar, touching her body and making her feel... *what... just what is Claire making me feel?* Nic knew the answer to the question, and it wasn't one she wanted to explore right now. She would think about it later, when she was alone and more in control of her emotions. Right now, she needed to get a bandage on her back and put a shirt on so she didn't feel so exposed and vulnerable.

Claire walked into the bathroom and stopped in the doorway to admire Nic's strong, stoic pose. She was bent over, running her hands through her hair. She wondered what she was thinking about. Looking at Nic, she noticed the side of an exposed breast and felt a tingle run through her body. *Oh, this is not good she thought. My husband has just died, they can't find his body and I am sitting here getting all worked up over a woman's body.* She took a deep breath to calm herself before walking into the bathroom. She was fighting a losing battle with her thoughts. She came up short when Nic turned around and the towel slipped, exposing both her breasts. Nic quickly yanked the towel back up, covering herself, but Claire saw the expression of mortification on her face.

Hoping to diffuse a heated situation by getting Nic's shirt back on Claire said, "So let's get your bandage on, shall we?"

She pulled out a box of medical supplies from the cabinet and took out all the things she would need to cover Nic's scar. She didn't have to look at Nic to know that Nic was looking at her, she could feel it. She was embarrassed to have been caught looking at Nic's breasts, especially since she had felt her own body respond so quickly. Returning to her seat on the toilet, she took out a pair of scissors and cut an oversized strip of gauze. She laid the strip over the scar and then went about cutting several lengths of tape to hold the gauze in place. She applied each piece of tape, making sure not to touch the graft and gently smoothing the tape down on Nic's back, and innocently enjoying the feel of Nic's back against her hand.

Nic could feel every stroke of Claire's fingers as she applied the bandage. Slowly she felt herself start to get aroused at Claire's touch. Nic knew she was treading on dangerous ground with this woman, but she couldn't help herself. Her body was betraying her at every touch. She had to bide her time until Claire was done and then she could get herself dressed and out of this compromising situation. Time was her enemy at this point though, and it seemed to drag with each stroke down her back, the touch of Claire's fingers sending chills throughout her body. It was a slow stroke along her rib cage that did her in.

She felt her heart speed-up, her nipples harden and her breath catch at the light contact along her breast. She heard Claire take a sudden gulp of air and her own sharp intake of breath gave away the fact that she too had felt the close contact.

"Oh, um... I, uh...."

"I— we're done here, aren't we?" It was more a statement than a question, as Nic stood and grabbed her t-shirt. She quickly donned the shirt and stepped away, hoping to put as much distance as she could between her and the person responsible for her over stimulated libido.

"Yes, of course, I'm sorry for… well you know. I mean, I didn't mean to touch … well you know what I mean." Claire motioned with her hands towards Nic's back as if she were giving some type of directions. Looking for a way out, she quickly gathered up the medical supplies.

"I should check on Grace while you get yourself together. Not that I mean you're not together or anything but… oh hell, I'm gonna check on my daughter. Come out when you're done." Claire looked like a sprinter heading for a second place finish as she left the bathroom and made her way back to the front room where Grace was still watching TV.

Nic started to laugh at Claire's obvious discomfort and suddenly knew she wasn't the only one feeling something. She felt herself relax as she regained her composure. She liked being in control and she was always in control. Control was power to Nic and she never gave up her power to anyone. She had learned at an early age to control her emotions. If her parents had taught her anything, it was that control meant power over people, or so they thought. Even if Claire was straight, it was good to know she wasn't the only one hot and bothered.

Nic left the bathroom feeling a little more like herself. When she entered the living room, she saw Claire holding Grace and whispering something in her daughter's ear. Grace shook her head animatedly, jumped down and ran to the kitchen.

Their eyes met briefly as Claire stood to follow her daughter into the kitchen. "Would you like to join us for dinner, Major?"

It was clear that Claire was trying to put some verbal distance between herself and the officer by using Nic's rank and it bothered Nic for some reason. Nic had kept her cool and didn't make a big deal out of the innocent touch. *Okay several touches,* Nic thought, but innocent nevertheless. She was beyond confused.

"Maybe I should go. I seem to have upset you for some reason and it would probably be better if I leave. Another time?"

"What? You think I am upset with you. What would I be upset with you for? No, no, I'm not upset with you at all, please…"

Nic inclined her head, waiting for Claire to continue.

"Look, it's not you, I assure you. Please, please stay for dinner and let me at least feed you since it was my daughter who jumped all over you and irritated your injury." Claire knew she was practically begging Nic to stay for dinner, partly out of guilt for what had happened with Grace and partly because she didn't want Nic to think that she had done something wrong.

"Peeese," Grace whispered as she grabbed Nic's leg and hugged it.

Reaching down she picked Grace up and said, "Okay. Since you asked so nicely, I guess I can stay a little longer." Smiling back at Claire, she gave the little girl a peck on the cheek and tossed her gently into the air. Grace squealed as she landed safely back in Nic's arms.

CHAPTER TEN

The conversation between the two, and sometimes Grace, was casual and innocent enough. They talked about their families, about the military and what made Nic want to join. They talked about people that they had in common and where certain people that Nic and Mike both knew were now. It surprised Claire to find out how many of the pilots that Mike had gone to flight school with were no longer alive. She had heard that the survival rate among pilots was average at best but with a war going on it was clear that being a helicopter pilot was much riskier that any other type of aviation. She wondered how those spouses survived after the loss of their loved one.

Dinner was starting to wind down and Grace was getting sleepy. She was starting to dip her little head closer and closer to her plate while she fought off sleep.

"Nic, would you mind sitting with Grace so I can start her bath?" She knew if she didn't act quickly Grace would be sleeping before she had her nightly ritual of bath and a bedtime story.

"I want to keep her routine as normal as possible," Claire said as she grabbed a bath towel and pajamas. "Pretty soon it will be chaos when Mike's family gets here."

"Sure, why not. We can sit on the couch and watch some TV and Grace can show me all her favorite shows. Right, Grace?"

"Kay," Grace said as she ran for the couch, making a dive right into the cushions as Nic followed. Claire watched as the two snuggled close.

"What do ya wanna watch, squirt?" Nic said, as she started surfing the channels.

"Cartoons," Grace yelled as she leaned closer to Nic.

Aw, how cute is that? Nic looks right at home with Grace. Claire felt warmth flow through her body at the sight.

"Hey, something age appropriate for a three year old. Okay?" Claire reminded.

Looking over at Claire, with something akin to a childlike grin on her face, she nodded and went back to channel surfing. If Claire didn't know better she would think that Nic had kids of her own, or perhaps she was just a big kid tucked under all of that camo.

"Nic?"

"Yeah?" Nic said watching the channels as they zoomed by.

"Have you ever thought about having kids? I mean, when you get married?"

"Aw," Nic handed the remote to Grace, "Wanna try it?" she said to Grace as she turned to Claire. "Well yeah, I mean I always thought eventually I would have kids and a family. I just haven't found the right person to make that kind of a commitment to." Nic hoped that she was being vague enough in her answer.

"You're great with Grace. I can see you with a whole pack of kids."

"Well, I don't know about a pack, but at least one or two." Nic watched as Claire finished clearing the table. She swallowed hard when Claire bent over the table to wipe up crumbs and her jeans pulled tight across a very nice and firm ass.

"I think you're gonna make a great mom, but that's just my opinion."

"Thanks." Nic decided to let the conversation end there. She didn't want to have to start explaining things about her life and she definitely didn't want to have that conversation with Claire when the sight of Claire cleaning the kitchen table turned her on.

Nic sat on the couch with Grace, the little girl cuddling next to her, and she wondered again what life would be like when she had a family of her own. She had always liked kids. In fact, she was the neighborhood babysitter when she was younger. She often spent at least one or two days a week watching a few of the neighbor kids while their parents went bowling or to dinner. She liked them and they liked her. She had a way with them, probably because she was the oldest of her siblings. It was an easier way to make a few bucks babysitting than mowing yards or washing cars. Not that she didn't do that too, but she liked babysitting much better. She looked down at Grace and wondered if she was partial to boys or girls. It was something she had never really thought about too much. If she had boys she could teach them how to play ball, skateboard or ride a bike, but then she realized she would teach a girl to do all of those things too. It didn't really matter to Nic whether she had boys or girls, as long as they were healthy.

Nic jumped when she heard a scream come out of the bathroom. Running, she practically ran into Claire, who was walking out of the bathroom sopping wet from the top of her head to her shoulders. Nic tried to peer under the wet hair that covered Claire's face.

"Are you ok? What happened?"

"Oh, I don't know. Someone pulled the plug up

on the faucet and the shower was active when I went to pour Grace's bath."

"Look, I don't remember pulling anything when I went to sit on the tub. Really," said Nic, pleading, but also beginning to laugh. It was clear that Claire was pissed but Nic couldn't help herself. Claire looked like a drowned rat and was dripping all over the floor in her haste to find the culprit who had pulled the lever.

"REALLY, I'm sure you don't know who did this, do you?" Claire said as she inched closer and closer to Nic who was now backed against the wall of the bathroom, nearly doubled over with laughter.

"So you think this is funny, do you?"

Moving into Nic she buried her wet hair into Nic's chest and began rubbing the soaking wet mess all over Nic's upper body. She grabbed Nic's shoulders and pulled their bodies together to make sure that Nic couldn't get away from the wet mess that she was creating. Laughing, she continued her onslaught even though Nic was now begging her, through great gulps of laughter, to stop.

Nic wrapped her arms around Claire to stop her from doing any more damage to her already wet t-shirt, and to keep her head from brushing against her breasts any further. Nic felt Claire's breasts make contact with her upper body as she moved back and forth. Holding Claire tighter she could feel her own nipples harden at the contact. She stood there with Claire in her arms inhaling her, a fragrance of freshness and heat, the kind of heat that comes from arousal.

Claire looked up into eyes that were clearly conveying a sensuality and lust she hadn't seen in a long time. She was so close to Nic she could feel Nic's breath on her face. Nic's scent made her head spin with desire, and the moment was too much for Claire to deny. Without thinking, she leaned forward and kissed Nic, first resting her lips gently against her, and when she felt Nic respond, she deepened the kiss.

Nic slid a hand up Claire's back and into her hair, pulling her closer to her lips. She heard a moan but wasn't sure whose it was. It didn't matter, she was on fire. She couldn't think clearly. It had been too long since she had been with someone and the depth of her need took her by surprise. It felt so good and she couldn't stop her body from reacting, from taking control of her brain. Her body tingled from the contact. She felt Claire's arms blocking her chest and wished she had moved her arms so she could feel Claire's nipples press against her own breasts. She pulled Claire's head back and exposed her neck to her lips. She started at Claire's earlobe and worked her way down to the raging pulse in her neck, licking, sucking and biting as she devoured Claire's neck. She heard Claire moan and it only served to spur her further down towards the hollow near Claire's collarbone.

"Mommy, you ok?"

As though they had been splashed by cold water they pulled apart. Claire took a step back and clutched her hands to her chest to cover her erect nipples, just in case Nic didn't already guess the damage that had been done by their contact. She struggled to control her breathing long enough so she could answer Grace.

"Yes, honey, mommy's ok. I just got a little wet when someone pulled the wrong plug in the bath that's all."

Nic couldn't pull her eyes away from the sight of Claire's generous curves beneath the t-shirt plastered to her skin. She flushed when she met Claire's smoldering gaze. Nic looked down to see her own hardened nipples pushing through her tight t-shirt.

Claire tossed Nic a towel. "Here. You might want to dry off. I need to change while Grace's bath runs. Would you mind?" She motioned to Grace with her chin as she sidestepped Nic, keeping her hands firmly over her breasts.

"Not at all. Come on little one. Let's sit on the couch and wait for mommy to get changed."

"But why? How did you get wet? And why was you kissing mommy? And why is mommy wet?" Nic suddenly realized that Grace was at that age where everything was a question. More importantly, Grace had seen everything between her and Claire. She wasn't sure how to answer so she decided to take the safe way out.

"You know what, Grace, why don't we let mommy answer those questions? OK?"

"Why?"

"Well, because ..."

"Because I am the mommy, that's why honey. And Nic has other things to do. Right Nic?" Claire said, saving Nic the embarrassment of having to try and explain something to a curious three year old. It was something she wasn't sure she could explain to herself. Claire gave Nic a half-hearted smile as she picked up Grace and took her into the bathroom.

She was being given a way out so Nic graciously accepted the offer, and grabbed her jacket from the back of the couch. She went to the door of the bathroom and briefly watched as Grace was lowered into the tub. Clearing her throat, she stuck her hands into her jeans and waited for Claire to turn around. When she didn't, Nic stood for a moment longer and then turned to leave.

"I better get going. I need to get to the office and check on things in Germany since it's almost morning over there. I'll call if I hear anything. Thanks again for dinner."

"Bye, Nic," said a soft little voice from the tub.

Smiling broadly Nic waved at Grace, "Bye cutie. See ya soon. Ok?"

"Kay."

"Good Night Nic." Claire didn't turn around, and her back was stiff.

"Good Night, Claire."

CHAPTER ELEVEN

Nic settled onto the seat of her motorcycle, and pulled her helmet on. She thought about what had just happened in the house. She suddenly realized that her body had reacted to someone's touch instead of to pain. Her body had turned a corner and was now reacting again to something completely out of the ordinary-the touch of another person.

She had battled for the last six months to get her body to a place where it no longer ached to walk, or hurt to get out of bed in the morning and get ready for work. To do things that everyone else took for granted everyday. She had put up with the ache in her hip and the jarring pain of her scar just to be able to ride her motorcycle again, because she wanted her life to feel somewhat normal. Now she was beginning to understand that her body and her mind were changing from fighting to survive to being able to enjoy something that had nothing to do with pain. That something was Claire.

She wanted to go back into the house and thank Claire for what had happened, but thought better of it as she realized that Claire might not know how to take the news of her dramatic change. In fact, she didn't think it would go over well with a straight woman. who, on top of everything else she was dealing with, may not want to find out that she had stimulated Nic into an epiphany.

Nic rode her bike back to her place feeling raw

and edgy. Try as she might, she couldn't get the vision of Claire's beautiful face, the feel of Claire's lips pressed wantonly against her own and the pressure of Claire's body fitting tightly against hers out of her head. She wondered briefly if she had imagined the whole thing, but her body reminded her that it was true. She was on fire. Changing course, Nic headed for the gym, knowing she was going to have to work through this physically before giving it anymore thought.

Heading for the locker room Nic could feel herself start to relax a little. By the time she came out, dressed and ready for a grueling workout, she had set her mind to the task at hand, which was to figure out what she was going to do about Claire. Sitting in the inverted leg press she started sorting through the facts as she could figure them out. Claire was a beautiful woman so it was easy to get lost in her beauty. She was exactly Nic's type too, so that didn't help the situation any. Had she said or done something to encourage Claire? *But Claire isn't gay!* Maybe the talk the two had earlier about Nic's accident in Iraq had something to do with what had happened. *But what?* Squeezing out the last of the reps, she racked her brain trying to think about what she might have done.

She switched machines and lowered her body into the hack machine. Her body ignited as she thought of Claire's gentle touch on her back as she changed the bandage. Claire's soft hands gently stroking the tape along the side of her breast was hard to ignore. She dropped down into the squat, straining as she pushed the weight back up into the start position. She could feel her legs trembling and wondered if it was the weight of the machine or her body responding as she remembered the innocent caresses.

Claire is in a vulnerable state and is just reaching out for comfort, that had to be it, she told herself as she changed to a different machine to work her hamstrings. A sense of relief replaced the anxiety that had been slowly building.

Of course, why didn't she see it sooner? Claire was reacting to the loss she was experiencing, and Nic was just the person that happened to be there when it all came to a head. There was that nagging thought again, *Claire isn't gay.* It would be one thing to reach out to another male for comfort, but a woman? She doubted anyone would make that kind of mistake, surely not a straight arrow like Claire. Perhaps the fact that Nic was a woman didn't enter into the picture. Maybe she was just someone who reminded Claire of Mike and so it would be easy to see how Claire could reach out in that way? Finishing her workout, she felt a sense of relief, tinged with a hint of disappointment.

One problem remained. Nic could convince her mind that it was innocent, but her body told her something else. Nic had reacted to Claire's advances and she felt completely captivated by her. *It's just 'cause I haven't been with someone in a while that's all. I'll get over it, no problem. We have a shared experience and that probably has something to do with it.* She definitely did not want to complicate things for herself or Claire, especially with what Claire was going through with Mike's body still missing. Her steely determination replaced the edginess she felt and she knew that she needed to remain professional with Claire, regardless of what had happened earlier. She could do this, she had to and once she put her mind to something it was all but a done deal as far as she was concerned. The issue was over and she was ready to move forward.

CHAPTER TWELVE

Claire sat with Grace, rocking her to sleep as she thought about the afternoon with Nic. *What happened between us?* She felt so out of control at that moment that she couldn't focus her mind on anything but Nic's body and how it felt to be held by her. It had been a long time since she had been intimate with anyone and today had awakened long dormant desires. She thought about Nic and wondered what she was thinking at that moment. Was Nic as unsettled by everything as she was? Was *she* thinking about their exchange in the bathroom, or did she play it off as a needy wife acting out? Claire needed to talk to Nic so she could explain, but she wasn't sure how she was going to do that. With the funeral and all of the things that needed to be handled in the next thirty days she wasn't sure she was going to be able to talk to the Major anytime soon.

Continuing to rock Grace, her thoughts wandered back to the feel of Nic's body, her slim muscular shape and how it made her feel to touch it. She imagined Nic lying next to her as Nic caressed her with soft, long strokes down her body, her skin tingling under the officer's touch. She felt herself tremble as she remembered how Nic felt under her touch, wishing she could feel that warm, soft body again. *Stop, this has to stop right now. No good will come from this kind of thinking. I need to focus on burying my husband and moving forward with my child,* Claire told herself, remembering how quickly Nic left after the sexually charged exchange.

I need to talk to someone about this. I don't think I can handle this kind of stuff right now. Claire put her sleeping daughter down and kissed her gently as she tucked her in tight. She had less than thirty days to make decisions and the last thing she needed was to lose focus by being sidetracked by a beautiful face.

"Hello Claire!" said the voice on the other end. "Are you OK? Have they found Mike?"

"Well, actually no." Claire suddenly wondered if it was a good idea to call Jordan after all. She felt her anxiety level rise at the thought of saying things out loud that she wasn't really ready to admit to herself as it was. But she was already on the phone and it was a little too late to second guess herself now. Besides, Jordan knew her like a book and would know if she was keeping something from her.

"Okay, what's wrong?" Jordan asked when Claire didn't say anything, "Grace! Is Grace all right?"

"Grace is fine. I just put her down to bed. Oh, I'm sorry for calling so late. Maybe I should just call you tomorrow, and we can talk then?"

"Oh no you don't, you know that it's never too late for you to call." Claire could hear the concern in Jordan's voice. "Look sweetie you know you can call anytime, day or night. What's going on? Are you all right?"

"Well ..." Claire hesitated, not knowing where to start.

"Yes?"

"Well, as a matter-of-fact something did happen tonight. Today in fact."

"Oh no, Is it bad Claire? Do you need me to get on a plane tonight?"

"No... it's not, bad really... well it's... well I..." She took a deep breath and tried to stop her hands from shaking.

"Relax, hon. Whatever it is we can get through this. Take a deep breath and just tell me what's happened. I can be there in a day if you need me right now."

Taking a deep breath again, she closed her eyes. It wasn't as easy to talk about it as she had hoped it would be.

"How long have we known each other, hon? Hmm, since forever, right? You can tell me anything. You know that, don't you? So shoot."

"Well, remember me telling you about the officer who came to the house to inform me of Mike's accident? She's really gone out of her way to help us with everything that has been going on here and well ... I kissed her tonight and I don't know what to do now." *There, I said it. It's out in the open and I can't take it back now. Jordan will know what to do.* Scared when she didn't hear anything on the other end of the line, Claire took a deep breath and tried again.

"Jordan? You still there?"

"Yeah, I think we might have a bad connection though. Did you just say what I think you said?"

"I'm afraid so. I kissed Major Caldwell tonight. Oh Jordan, what am I going to do now?" Claire felt like she was going to break down any moment and her voice gave away her secret as she continued talking to Jordan. "It happened so fast and before I knew what I was doing it was over with. Oh god, it felt so good. I'm screwed, aren't I?"

"Okay sweetie, hold on and tell me exactly what happened. It isn't everyday that you just kiss a total stranger. Besides, does Major Caldwell know about you?"

"Look, I don't even know if Nic, I mean, Major Caldwell, is gay, let alone if she knows anything about me and Mike. I mean I doubt she knows anything, and besides she isn't a total stranger. We have sort of known each other since college." Claire told her long time friend about the events that had happened in the last few days and how she knew Nic. Before long Jordan knew everything that had happened all the way down to the little detail of how Nic's body felt under Claire's touch.

"Shit, kid this is something. One day you're a widow, the next you're groping the body of a hot female officer. Geez, leave it to you to get all the breaks." Claire knew Jordan was making light of the situation for her benefit, and the effort made her smile.

"God Jordan, please, this is bad. What am I going to do?"

"Well did she say anything when she left? I mean how did she act? Was she weirded out or did she act normal?"

"Actually she was pretty calm about the whole thing."

"You mean she acted like this kinda thing happened to her all of the time?"

"Well, not exactly. I sort of dismissed her. She said she had things that needed to be taken care of at the office and thanked me for dinner and left. Oh god, I was awful to her because I was so embarrassed about what happened. I should call and apologize to her." Frantic, all Claire could think to do was hang up the phone and call Nic to apologize for her behavior.

"WAIT, wait, wait... calm down, Claire. Just take a deep breath and let's think this thing through. You have been through so much in the past few days that it is probably normal that you would act differently than expected. She has probably seen worse behavior that she can't explain, especially in situations like this. You just might make things worse if you call and bring this all out again. Besides, you said she reacted to your touch, too, didn't you? So maybe she doesn't want to be reminded of her reaction either? Even if it was as innocent as you said it was." Jordan's voice was calm and certain.

"Look, maybe the best thing to do right now is to ignore what happened, to just let it lie and not give it too much attention. You've been put through a tragedy that most women will never experience so it is to be expected that you might act out due to the stress and the loss you have gone through. Right?"

"Oh God, I guess your right. I'm just so confused and stressed I can't seem to think straight right now. So much has happened and I don't know which way is up anymore. I guess I just read more into Major Caldwell doing her job and put her in a difficult situation." Claire was trying to spin the situation differently in her mind but it still felt the same to her. She was attracted to Nic and couldn't deny it.

"Look, I can be there in a day and we can get through all of this stuff together. Why..."

"No, no. Why don't we wait until we know more about Mike? That way, you will be here when the really difficult stuff happens, you know? Mike's family and the funeral. I'm sure his mom is going to want to make all the arrangements and I am going to need someone in my court when she gets here. Okay?" Claire interrupted, hoping that her friend would give her a little time to clear her mind before the real issues arrived.

"Sure, but promise me you will call if anything, and I mean anything, happens."

"I promise, and thanks again for listening and being the voice of reason. I don't know what I would do without you, Jordan."

"Sure you do. You would drive on just like you are now. Just a little faster, that's all. I love you, hon, and make sure you kiss Grace for me and tell her Aunty Jordan can't wait to see her. Okay?"

"Sure. See you soon."

Claire rolled over, putting the phone back on Mike's side of the bed and laid her head on his pillow. His scent had long evaporated from the pillowcase, not that Claire ever felt the need for his scent. She did find it somewhat relaxing to know that Grace had a father that loved her and he was always a good husband, at least in the ways that mattered to her. No, she was wrong. She would miss Mike, his strength, his kindness, and his friendship. But now she had to find her own strength, a strength that she hadn't had to draw upon for some time. In a crisis of faith or loss, people either stepped up and met the challenge or they collapsed in its wake. Claire knew she had to rise up out of it and step up boldly meeting it head on, not only for her sake but for her daughter's as well.

CHAPTER THIRTEEN

Nic could feel the heat of the body next to hers. The slender brunette lay there panting from the lust that had ensued just moments earlier. Nic trembled from the orgasm rolling through her. Yet, even as the final tremors subsided, she wanted more. More tension. More pressure. She rolled toward the back that was exposed to her and moved her hips to make contact with the woman's smooth, firm ass. Nic gasped as her nipples raked her companion's back and instantly hardened again. She ran her tongue along the brunette's neck, enjoying the sweet taste of lust disguised as sweat. Her muscles tensed in a shudder of anticipation. She ran her hand over a narrow shoulder and down an arm that felt slight compared with her own.

Inhaling the scent of clean hair and hot skin, Nic willed herself to remember every moment as if it would be her last with this exotic stranger. Her companion's fingers tightened and she undulated against Nic's hips, moaning softly. Nic started to feel the familiar tingle of another orgasm and, slipping free of the woman's grasp, she grabbed the hips in front of her and began to grind slowly into them, rubbing her already hardened clit into the firm ass. Her nipples added more fuel to the fire as they rubbed against her sexy partner's back. Her breathing started to quicken and she knew it would only be a matter of seconds before she came again. She wanted to prolong this feeling as long as she could, but her body wanted something else.

Nic heard gasps as the woman pushed harder against her, brown hair thrown back onto her shoulder. The woman was begging for release, each plea more insistent. Reaching around her, Nic grasped her nipples and gently tugged them into erect points. Nic slid her other hand into the slick folds between her lover's legs and entered her. The beautiful woman adjusted her legs so Nic could enter deeper, and as she slid her fingers in as deep as she could she felt her hand being pushed even further.

"Hard baby, I want you to fuck me harder." The silky voice commanded as she helped Nic work her hand in and out of her wet pussy.

"That's it baby. Oh god you're gonna make me come again."

Nic felt her quiver as an orgasm formed. Her own body reacted, beginning its own orgasmic dance with her companion's. She worked her hips harder, and felt Claire reach between them and stroke her clit, then slide her hand between her legs and enter Nic swiftly.

Spreading her legs, she accepted the long thrusts and prolonged her orgasm a few moments longer before turning away from the woman she had just made love with.

A buzzing broke through the sounds of their labored breathing and continued to demand attention until, finally, Nic pressed her head into the pillows to kill its incessant scream and reached for the alarm clock.

God, it was just a dream, another Goddamn dream. This time it felt so real, so fulfilling. She had dreamt of Claire for nights and the outcome was always the same- a gut wrenching orgasm that left her both satisfied and aching for the real thing.

###

Nic had opted not to see Claire after their last encounter, afraid of the embarrassment that it would bring them and the unanswered urges it would cause. She asked the sergeant to call to find out if Claire needed anything and to let her know that there were no new developments. It was all the Major could do not to stop by and see her or pick up the phone and talk to Claire. Instead, she mailed the forms they had never gotten around to, with a Post-em telling Claire to call if she needed help with them. She knew she was torturing herself thinking about Claire, but she couldn't control her dreams. She stayed later at the office using the excuse that she was cleaning up paperwork. She was even working out at the gym for two hours instead of one so that she was exhausted when she got home. Even riding her motorcycle was offering no relief to the face she saw every time she closed her eyes. She had it bad and she knew it, but she also knew no good could come from it.

Swinging her feet to the floor Nic rested her head in her hands and tried to fend off the approaching headache. The stress was getting to her and there was little she could do right now to fix things for herself or for Claire. Finding Mike's body was paramount to getting out of this situation with Claire. When they could close this chapter, Claire would move out of base housing and be on her way, and Nic would be back focusing on another family in their hour of crisis. She cursed herself for letting the Priest talk her into taking on Captain Monroe's family personally. She knew better than to become personally involved. She limped to the shower and waited until it had time to warm up to its hotter than hot temperature, just the way she liked it. She slid into the pulsating jets and she leaned her head back into them to try and relieve some of the tension that had settled into her neck and shoulders from the headache. She knew she was going to have to try a different approach to forget Claire. Perhaps it was time for some company to take her mind off her problems. The weekend was coming and she deserved a little time away from the base. Maybe she would drive into San Diego and hit up a gay bar?

CHAPTER FOURTEEN

Claire heard the knocking at the door and rolled over to see what time it was. *Geez, 6:30 in the morning? What idiot would be knocking at my door at this hour?* Grabbing her robe, she headed for the front door and looked through the peephole.

"Jordan!" she yelled as she unlocked the door and hugged her friend. "What the heck are you doing here?" The two friends hugged until a little voice interrupted them.

"Mommy, what you doing?" Grace asked, still sleepy and rubbing her eyes.

"Awww, honey, did Aunty Jordan wake you up?"

"Yep."

"Aw, I'm sorry. Come here sweetie and let me take a look at you and then you and me can cuddle on the couch while mommy makes us some breakfast. Okay?"

Nodding, Grace raised her arms as Jordan dropped her bags inside of the house. Turning to Claire she stuck her tongue out and said, "See, she wants her Auntie Jor. Oh and I'll take waffles. Are waffles okay with you, Grace?" Jordan looked down at her goddaughter and laughed when the small child perked up.

"Yeah, waffles. My favorite."

"Good. Let's sit down and let me look at you. It seems like years since I've seen you, Grace. Look how big you've gotten. How old are you again?"

Raising three fingers, Grace smiled and counted

off her fingers.

"Wow, you really have gotten older, haven't you?" Jordan said. Grace and Jordan babbled on the couch as Claire started the coffee and looked for the waffle iron. She chuckled as she thought about her friend showing up unannounced, knowing that it had probably taken Jordan hours to find a flight. Jordan always knew how to read Claire and this time was no exception. If truth be told, Claire was glad her best friend had shown up without having to be asked. She needed someone, and right now she couldn't think of anyone she wanted around more than Jordan. Well maybe a tall, roguishly good-looking female officer would be nice, too, but Nic was exactly why she was glad Jordan had shown up. Her friend would help her put things into perspective and keep them there.

"Here you go, morning glory," Claire said as she passed the hot mug of coffee to her overly chipper friend. "Next time how about a little notice?"

"If I had told you I was coming, you would have just told me not to, and I could tell by your tone the other night that you needed someone. We both know whom that someone might turn out to be if you're not careful. Right?" She lifted her eyebrows and winked. "Besides, I have tons of personal time stocked up at work, so I just left Carol a message and told her not to expect me for a while. They know how hard I work the rest of the year so they can cut me some slack."

"Well I just don't want you to get into any hot water over me. I would have called you when we found something out about Mike."

"I know, sweetie." She clasped Claire's hand and looked over at Grace. "Besides, it gives me a chance to spend time with my only goddaughter slash niece.

Right, honey? You want to spend time with Auntie Jor while mommy relaxes, don't you?" Jordan bounced Grace on her knees. "Besides, I want to see this woman who is making you swoon before all of the stressful stuff starts and family is swarming around. So, relax. I can run interference if she shows up and give you some time to work a few things out. I am sure you have tons to do with Mike's affairs and I can watch Grace while you take care of things. Okay?"

Claire knew Jordan was right. She hadn't had any time to try and work through Mike's affairs, and time was ticking on her stay in housing. Better to tie up those things that she could now so when things did get harried at least she would know she had the rest taken care of. Although Nic had said she would help with the arrangements, she hadn't heard from her in several days. Clearly, she had decided to distance herself. Although Claire had to admit she was disappointed, she certainly couldn't blame Nic for it.

"You're right. I could use some time to myself to get things in order. Once the families get here it will be chaos at best. Thanks for coming, Jordan. I really do appreciate it, even if you did get us up way too early." Shoving her friend with her shoulder she went back into the kitchen to work on the waffles.

CHAPTER FIFTEEN

Nic bent over and bloused her boots, putting the blousing tie under the pant leg and tucked the pants neatly above her desert combat boots. She missed the days of spit-shined black combat boots that gave her uniform that polished look. She felt like the desert boots were dirty looking and always needed a cleaning. She took pride in her appearance and it showed from the way she wore her BDUs. She liked the way she felt in her uniform, commanding and strong, and now her body was starting to feel that way, too. She entered the office vaguely aware of someone waiting off to her left.

"Father, how are you?"

"Well Nic. How are you getting along?"

"Fine, Sir. Come on back to my office. Can I get you something to drink?"

"No thanks. I just had breakfast and thought, since I was in the neighborhood, I would stop by. By the way, how is Mrs. Monroe doing? I heard that there was some sort of mix-up with Captain Monroe's body. Is that true?" Wiping his brow with a handkerchief he took from his pocket, he followed her down the bland corridor.

"I am afraid so, Father. It seems that someone screwed up in Germany and they can't find him. For all we know he may still be in Iraq somewhere, but no one seems to know anything." Shaking her head at the absurdity of it all, she continued into her office, closing the door behind her.

"You don't by any chance have a clergy member over there that you can call to see if last rites were given, do you?" she asked, hoping that the Priest could lend some much needed divine intervention on behalf of the Monroe family.

"I can make a few calls and see what I can find out. The fact that Capt. Monroe wasn't Catholic doesn't mean he wasn't given some type of service over there before being shipped back. Let me see what I can do. How is Mrs. Monroe holding up?" he asked as he sat in the seat opposite Nic.

"To be honest, Father, I haven't seen her in a couple of days. I have been pretty busy with a few more informs and I didn't want to call her until I had something more promising to tell her. I just hadn't anticipated it would take this long," she said looking down at her paperwork, hoping to avoid the knowing eyes of the priest.

"Tell you what. Why don't I make a few calls and give you a call this afternoon if I find something out? We just need to give Mrs. Monroe some closure so that she can move on with her life." He stood and extended his hand. "I'll see what I can do, Major."

"Thank you, Father. I would really appreciate that and I am sure Mrs. Monroe would, also."

"Nic?"

"Yes, Father?"

"If you need someone to talk to, I am always around, you know?" He looked into Nic's eyes. "I wanted you to know that, just in case."

Embarrassed, she let her hand drop to her side and nodded. "Thanks, Father. I'll remember that."

"Well, I know you knew the Captain and his wife. Please give her my best when you see her," he said as he turned to the door to leave. "You know, Nic, God loves all his flock regardless of how they live their lives. We should not judge someone just because *they* might be different. Not that I think you judge anyone, but just in case you heard something that might make you avoid Mrs. Monroe. What she needs right now is our support and our prayers."

Puzzled, but unwilling to admit her ignorance on the matter, she simply nodded. "I understand Father. I will make sure I stop and see her this weekend."

The priest left and his words echoed over and over in her head. *Just because they might be different.* Different how? How could Claire possibly be different? Did she cheat on Mike? Was she married before Mike? Was the priest talking about some cardinal sin Claire had committed? What could possibly make Claire different?

Nic looked down at her watch. It was only a few more hours before she could call it a week and head downtown to catch some nightlife. She looked at the phone and debated on whether to call Claire to see how she was doing, but all Nic could think of was that brown hair, her warm scent and those eyes. She closed her eyes and remembered the kiss in the bathroom, completely inappropriate but so intoxicating. A warm shiver went down Nic's body at the thought and she could feel her BDU's pressing against her hardened nipples. Trying to take a deep breath in hopes of clearing her mind only made her nipples harder as they rubbed against the stiff cloth, prolonging her agony.

That's it. I'm going out tonight and getting laid, she thought as she readjusted her uniform in hopes of finding some relief from the torture she was putting herself through. Grabbing her cap she made a decision. Tonight she was going to find a buxom, leggy brunette and get lost in her. She made her way toward the door and gave the sergeant some last minute instructions about how she should be contacted if they located Capt. Monroe, and a flip remark about not being contacted about anything else.

CHAPTER SIXTEEN

"Claire, what do you think about going out tonight?" Jordan asked. "Just you and me, sushi and sake, no baby, and no Major Gorgeous."

"I don't know, Jordan. I should be here if they find Mike. It wouldn't look right. I mean, me going out when I have yet to deal with Mike's death." Claire wished they would find Mike so she could deal with the loss and the final steps of closing out her life with the military. She didn't want to sound crass, but she felt like her life was in limbo until he was found.

"Look, I talked to your neighbor and she agrees. It would do you good to get out and away from all of this. Trust me, you aren't getting away from your problems, you're just escaping a little and everyone understands a friend wanting to help her best friend get a bit of space from all of it." Jordan took Claire's hands in her own. "She said she would come over whenever we were ready to leave and take Grace over to her house. When was the last time Grace got to go out and play? It has to be hard on her, too."

Claire nodded in agreement. Grace didn't understand what was going on because she was used to Mike not being around. Their lives had to be separate from Mikes because he was constantly gone somewhere, with some unit that needed aviation support. She knew that when she married him and that was what made the decision to marry him easy. He would rarely be home and she would truly have her own life without the headache of having a husband. Now, she regretted those thoughts. Mike had deserved better.

"Come on." Jordan's pleading expression made Claire laugh. "We can spend some girl time and remember the good times we had in college. I can't guarantee it will be fun but it will definitely give you a break from all of this."

Claire let out a long, audible sigh. It had been a rough last couple of days and she couldn't think straight right now.

"Okay, tell you what. We can go have dinner but we need to get back early. Okay? I don't want to leave Grace for too long."

"Okay. Why don't we just play it by ear and see what happens. Deal?"

"Come on, Jordan. I agreed to go to dinner. Isn't that enough?"

"I know, sweetie, but someone has to look out for you because you won't. So just let me work out tonight and see where it leads. Compromise?"

"Fine." Claire sighed. "You win."

"A shallow victory, I assure you."

"Somehow I doubt it. You like to win and I hate to give up control and you know it. So enjoy it while you have it because it won't last." Giving Jordan a faint smile, Claire turned and walked to her room to change.

Nic rushed home, peeled off her uniform, removed the gauze and tape from her back, and jumped into a hot shower. Trying to cleanse both her mind and her body, she let the hot water cascade down her body. She was ready for a relaxing dinner, a few drinks and a night of cruising at one of the gay bars downtown. It had been a long time since she had been out and she was suddenly looking forward to the local action. She felt her body start to key up at the mere thought of the chase, or, god forbid, being touched again. Nic hadn't had time to think about women, let alone try and seduce one. The incident with the female driver the previous week had reminded her she was healing rather nicely. Tonight was different though. Tonight she was on the prowl, and she was looking for a nice diversion. Something long and lanky to make her forget what she couldn't have.

An hour later, Nic was downtown sitting at a sports bar waiting for the gay bar to open, sipping ale while watching the local college team get their butts handed to them by a top ranked division one team. Closing her eyes, she leaned her head back and took a deep breath as she felt herself relax with each sip of her beer. Deciding to stay where she was she waved down the bartender and ordered a burger.

###

Claire felt the warm sake slide effortlessly down her throat and warm her body. Exhaling, she let a small smile escape her lips as she looked across the table at her friend.

"I guess you were right Jor. I needed this. I just didn't know how much until now."

"I know. That's why your friends are more like family than your family is. Who knows you better than me?" asked Jordan, winking at Claire. "Besides, having dinner with a hot chick always takes my mind off my troubles."

"Well, let me know when she gets here and I'll invite her to have dinner with us."

"You better be nice. It's a long walk back to base."

"Aw, you know I think you're hot, just not my type."

"Well you're not my type either, just for the record," Jordan said. "Besides, I don't date women with ready-made families. Too much baggage, but I might make an exception for that little cutie at home. She loves her Auntie Jor."

"We all love Auntie Jor, just not like that," said Claire enjoying the light banter with her best friend.

"Yea, yea, you girls are all alike. 'wine me, dine me, just don't date me'." Jordan laughed as she took another sip of her sake.

"Somehow I don't think you have a problem getting dates or finding attractive women to date. Right?"

"Well the pool is evaporating. A lot of women are settling down and nesting. I guess I am just not the nesting type right now. Maybe in a year or two when I'm 40, but right now why not be like Jesus and love 'em all."

Claire knew Jordan didn't believe the rhetoric she was spouting but she was friend enough to indulge Jordan's fantasy. Jordan wanted nothing more than to settle down and be monogamous, but she was putting on a good face for Claire. Sometimes friendship was about what they didn't say than what they did.

"Gosh, I haven't had sushi in so long," Claire said, changing the subject before it landed on something she didn't want to talk about yet.

CHAPTER SEVENTEEN

The Pussy Cat bar was a gay bar most of the month and every third Friday it was transformed into a lesbian bar. It lacked the finesse of the lesbian bars back East, replaced by black walls, non-existent lighting, and music with the bass so loud you could feel it through the floor. It seethed raw energy, the kind given off by baby dykes who had missed the whole 80's scene with its drug induced frenzy and free loving women.

Nic entered the bar. She couldn't help but notice the crowd. It was either a very young crowd or she was getting too old to be hanging out at the bars. Probably a little bit of both. No matter. She was in the mood for cruising and she didn't mind a baby dyke to take her mind off a certain brunette. The energy in the bar was almost palpable. It wrapped around Nic enveloping her, stroking her like a hand roughly caressing her, and she felt her body tighten as she thought about the chase that was about to begin. Ordering a beer, she scoped out the women standing around the perimeter of the dance floor. Some were in baggy jeans and the latest T-shirt from the men's store at the mall. That wasn't what Nic was looking for. She liked feminine women so she focused on them.

She looked around, but since no one caught her eye, she wandered into the back room. The change in music and atmosphere was immediate. The techno music was gone, replaced with top 40's and danceable eighties songs. Nic could never figure out what the younger generation saw in techno, but then she was sure her parents couldn't figure out what she saw in rock when they were die-hard country fans.

Nic spotted an empty booth in a dark corner and slid in. She watched as an older crowd started to fill the tables on the outside of the dance floor. From her vantage point, she could see everything in the club. Not only was the crowd a bit older, but they were teaming with femmes of all shapes and sizes. Since she was here for one thing and one thing only she made it a point to notice where all the cute women were seated. She made a mental note of who came with someone and who came with a group of people. She didn't want to tangle with a pissed off girlfriend.

She hadn't been a player before the accident but she had always made time for a beautiful woman on the weekends. She was careful to explain the situation before she ever got started for the night and if the girl wasn't willing to play by the rules, Nic moved on. She wasn't in a position to make promises her job wouldn't allow her to keep and that was her out with women who wanted more. Nic watched as a couple of blondes stood at the bar, cruising the crowd. They reminded Nic of Claire as they shyly met her glance.

Nice bodies, great legs, and lips that beg to be kissed.

Nic wasn't much into blondes. She loved brunettes though, the kind of mousy brown hair that Claire had. Nic closed her eyes as she thought about what it would be like to run her hands through Claire's hair as she made love to her. She thought about how soft those lips would feel as she ran her tongue over them before she parted them for a kiss. Nic felt her body tighten at the thought of running her tongue along Claire's throat as she kissed her neck. She wondered how Claire's nipples would feel when her thumb brushed over them, hardening at her touch. Nic imagined how she would stand behind Claire and run her hands over the front of her body, caressing her breasts as she brushed her hardened clit into her ass. Nic was a top and she loved a woman like a top, dominating a woman with her size and prowess. She thought about how Claire would moan as she reached down Claire's body, parting her legs and stopping at the wet folds Nic wanted to enter. Nic felt herself tremble at the thought of Claire begging her to make love to her.

Christ, what was she doing? She came here to get away from thinking of Claire and here she was fantasizing about her. Would every woman tonight make her think of Claire? Did she have it that bad for Claire that she couldn't escape her even for a few hours? Nic stopped the waitress and ordered two more beers. She needed to get her mind off Claire, and right now, she needed a diversion.

Claire and Jordan entered the Pussy Cat bar just as a line started to form outside.

"Look, Jor, I'm not so sure this is a good idea," yelled Claire over the techno beat.

"Oh, come on. Just for an hour. You promised. Besides, how long has it been since you have been around some family?" Jordan peered down the bar, smiling at a butch leaning against a column.

"Today."

"Huh?"

"You asked me when the last time was I was around some family and I said today," Claire said as she followed Jordan's gaze down the bar.

"Oh, you know what I meant, Claire. Our kinda family." Jordan met the eyes of the tall butch as a cute femme came over and slipped her arms around the woman. The butch winked in Jordan's direction and hugged the girl close to her body. Jordan raised her beer in the direction of the woman and smiled, then turned to face Claire.

"Gee, shot down already, Jor?"

"She wasn't that cute anyway. Besides, I like 'em a little more girly if you know what I mean," she said as she raised her eyebrows at Claire.

"Don't get any ideas, Jordan. We don't have that kinda friendship. No benefits here sister."

"I know, I know, but hey a girl can always hope, can't she?"

"No, a girl can't always hope. We decided a long time ago we were better friends than we would ever be lovers. Remember that conversation, Aunty Jor?" Claire liked to remind Jordan of the promise she made to Claire when they were back in college. She would never cross the line from best friend to girlfriend regardless of the circumstances. Even though Jordan had been drunk when she made the promise, Claire still held her to it.

"Fine. There are lots of cute women in here and if I can't find at least one, then I am giving up on women, forever," Jordan said as she scanned the room looking for Ms. Right Now.

"That's a little dramatic, even for you, Jordan. I'm sure that you'll have women dripping off of you in about 10 minutes. You always do." Claire looked around the room, hoping that this would be a quick hour, and she could just go home and be with Grace. Claire regretted promising Jordan she would spend at least an hour at the bar. She wasn't ready, and the thumping music was already giving her a headache.

"Hey, will you watch my drink while I go to the ladies room? I think that sake is going right through me." Jordan was already asking the bartender for directions by the time Claire agreed. Claire sat and watched the mating dance of the baby dykes as they strutted back and forth in front of the women hugging the walls. She noticed that they all pretty much looked like they shopped at the same men's store, opting for baggy jeans, oversized logoed T-shirts and short spiky hair. God, was she glad that she wasn't coming out into this crowd. She didn't find anything sexy about the new look the dykes were sporting. She preferred someone a little more polished. Someone who exuded self-confidence, even a bit of cockiness. Someone like Nic Caldwell.

Claire rolled her eyes as she realized she was thinking about Nic again. What was it about this woman that she couldn't get her out of her mind? Mike's body wasn't even home yet, and here she was thinking about Nic as if she was an option. *I need to get out of here. All of this estrogen must be having an effect on me. All I can think about is a sexy, hot woman who may or may not be gay.* Claire looked around hoping that she would see Jordan so they could get the hell out of there.

Jordan was walking towards the bathroom when she noticed the good looking woman sitting in a booth by herself. Jordan slowed down as she got closer and threw the woman a smile that sent most women to their knees. Jordan waited until she got a return glance and smile from the woman and then nonchalantly sauntered past.

Nic was finishing her second beer when she spotted the cute brunette looking at her as she walked in her direction. She was familiar, but Nic couldn't quite put her finger on why. Maybe she had seen her around before, or maybe she worked at the base. It didn't matter. It was clear that the woman was trying to send her signals, but she wasn't sure she was interested. Nic's two beers from dinner and the two she had just consumed were catching up to her so she decided she better relieve herself before the club got any busier and she lost her great vantage point of the dance floor. She had motioned the waitress over and asked her to keep an eye on her last beer, dropping a $5 on her tray to keep her interested.

Nic made her way to the line for the bathroom. She couldn't help but notice the cute brunette from earlier standing a few feet in front of her, looking right at her. She smiled at the brunette as she took her place in the long line. *Why did bars always have the worst bathrooms for women? Geez the men never have to wait in line.* Nic wasn't against going into the men's bathroom if she was desperate, but the view was great from where she was standing. Nic watched as the cute brunette made conversation with someone else in line, although her gaze never left Nic's face. Smiling back at the woman, Nic watched as she ended her conversation and walked towards her.

"Hey, tall, dark and gorgeous. I couldn't help but notice you were sitting alone at your table. Are you waiting for someone?" Jordan asked, as she looked Nic up and down.

"Well that's original. Do you use that line very often?" Nic chuckled, hoping she didn't sound too jaded. She looked at the beautiful woman and knew for sure she had seen her before, but she just couldn't remember where. It definitely wasn't in her bed. Nic would have remembered.

"What, you don't like the compliment?" Feigning hurt, Jordan moved closer to Nic.

"Well let's just say that I've heard that same line in the past week," Nic said as she watched the bold woman close the distance between them. *Hmm, seduction,* thought Nic. She was definitely feeling this woman's energy rub off on her.

"Besides, I think you can do better than that, can't you?" Nic said rather huskily as she bent her head down and whispered it in Jordan's ear.

"My actions speak louder than my words ever could."

"Well, I like a woman who knows what she wants and isn't afraid of being shot down. So let me ask you, are you here alone?" Nic hoped the answer was yes but doubted the beautiful woman was ever alone.

"Actually...."

There it was, Nic thought. She had a girlfriend and was most likely a player. She straightened up and looked down at Jordan with a cynical look.

"Now wait, let me explain," Jordan said as she recognized the beginnings of a brush off.

"I am here with a friend, but not a girlfriend," she said as she put girlfriend in air quotes.

"Okay. So friend with benefits?" Nic asked, hoping to make small work of this situation. She didn't want to invest any more time if she wasn't going to get anywhere with her.

"Oh hell no. I actually had to drag her down here. She is going through some stuff and I just wanted to get her out and away from everything. It's been a while since she's been around *family*, if you know what I mean. I thought this might give her a break from her problems."

"Well, she is lucky to have such a caring friend."

"Yeah, well, I'm not sure she sees it that way. By the way, my name is Jordan. Yours?"

Claire was sitting on the bar stool trying to fend off the latest advances from a soft butch who thought Claire was absolutely adorable, or so she told Claire. Claire couldn't remember the last time a woman had hit on her and she wasn't as uncomfortable with the process as she thought she would be, but right now she was in a different place. She looked around hoping to see Jordan somewhere, anywhere, but she didn't and she was losing patience quickly.

"Look, I appreciate the compliment but I'm here with someone and if you're still here when she gets back she might be pissed," Claire said, hoping that the baby dyke would take the not too subtle hint.

"Well all I have to say is she's an idiot to leave someone so beautiful here all by herself. Why don't I just sit here and keep you company until she gets back. It'll give us time to get to know each other better."

Claire had had it. She stood, ran a hand through her hair and shrugged. "Thanks, but I'll just go and see what is keeping her. Please don't bother getting up. I think I can find my way to the bathroom all by myself. Besides, I think that cute little blonde over there was checking you out," she said, pointing in the direction of an unknowing blonde across the room. The dyke turned to look and Claire made a beeline for the other dance room and the bathrooms located there. She turned the corner and spotted Jordan talking to a woman whose back was to Claire.

"I knew it," Claire whispered, as she made her way closer to the couple.

Claire could see Jordan laughing at something the taller woman whispered in Jordan's ear. She also noticed the way Jordan was running her hand up and down the arm of the unsuspecting woman. Claire had seen Jordan at work before and this poor woman didn't stand a chance with her friend. Once Jordan made physical contact with her prey, it was over. It was the one sure sign Claire knew that Jordan was in kill mode. Claire was done with the bar scene tonight and she was leaving with or without Jordan.

Claire was going in to extract her friend and she would just have to apologize later for the tactic. She wanted to leave this meat market and she knew Jordan wouldn't take no for an answer. Claire walked up to Jordan and stepped between the two women with her back to the stranger.

"Look, honey," Claire said as she ran her hands up Jordan's arms, "we need to get home. If we spend any more time here you won't want to get busy later." Leaving all of the innuendo hanging in her voice, Claire used her body language to try and convince the stranger behind her that she was in fact Jordan's girlfriend.

"Claire," both Nic and Jordan said in unison, one out of surprise, and the other out of anger.

Claire stood transfixed looking at Jordan, hoping against hope that the voice behind her was not who she thought it was.

"I'm sorry. Do you know Claire?" Jordan asked the woman she had been flirting with for the last ten minutes.

Claire turned and looked up into the face she hoped was only a dream but what she saw pulled her back into reality.

"Nic."

"You two know each other?" Jordan asked as she looked at both women who were now visibly shaken. "Wait, wait. Let me get this straight. This is *the* Nic Caldwell, *the* Major Nic Caldwell?" Jordan said, waiting for an answer from either of the two blushing women.

"Jordan, we need to go, NOW." Claire turned and walked towards the front door of the bar.

"Well, nice to meet you, Nic. I have heard so much about you. Sorry we didn't get a chance to become better acquainted, but somehow, I think we might in the near future," Jordan said as she backed away from a confused Nic.

Panting, Claire keyed the lock and practically started the car before she closed the door. Jordan had to move quickly or she was going to be left behind.

"Hey, slow down and let me get in, Claire."

"Fuck, fuck, fuck. Why did I let you talk me into going with you tonight, shit," Claire said as she rested her head on the steering wheel at a stoplight.

"How could I be so fucking stupid? Oh God." Claire was in full panic mode and she started to shake as she rolled the window down to let cold air into the car. She could feel her heart pounding so loud it reverberated in her ears, and pulsed in her eyes. She was outed and not by her own doing.

"Oh God, what am I going to do now? Shit, shit,

shit."

Jordan reached over and grabbed Claire's hands hoping to still them and her head.

"Look, I am sure Nic isn't exactly going to be blabbing about seeing you at a lesbian bar. She would be outing herself, too. Remember? Don't ask, don't tell. At least we know that she's a lesbian for sure now," Jordan said with a grin. Claire wasn't amused and she glared at Jordan, angry at her best friend for making her go to the bar tonight.

CHAPTER EIGHTEEN

What the hell just happened? thought Nic as she slid back into the booth. One minute she was thinking about breakfast plans with a beautiful woman, the next she was watching Claire Monroe call the same woman 'Honey' and promising something about an intimate night later. Claire and honey together? Shit, what the hell was going on and why was Claire in a gay bar with this woman? Nic felt like she had just walked into the middle of a movie with no idea what the plot was. She was in a state of shock as she played the last five minutes over and over in her head. Had Claire really just called the cute woman 'Honey'? Nic didn't know whether she wanted to puke or jump for joy at seeing Claire at the lesbian bar.

Nic made her way out of the club, waving assent at a couple that indicated their interest in the booth. She needed air. What she really wanted were some answers but that wasn't going to happen right now, not in the condition she was in. Shock wouldn't even begin to describe her feelings. No, it was more akin to betrayal. Here she was wishing the woman she had been thinking about for the past week and a half was gay and now not only was she gay but she was already with someone. *Christ could this get any worse?*

She wrestled her keys from her pants pocket, practically ripping her jeans before getting them free and getting the car door open. Sitting in her Jeep, she stared out the window, seeing Claire's face when she had turned around. The shocked look on Claire's face when she realized who was standing behind her. Nic realized the implications of what Claire had seen and the realization hit her like a punch to the stomach.

"Shit, I was just caught in a gay bar. Great. What else can happen?" Nic asked herself as she buried her face in her hands. She sat there for a moment trying to figure out what she should do next. Go to her commander and resign her commission? No, there was no way Claire would out her like that. Would she? Nic remembered the kiss the two of them had shared at Claire's house. What if Claire thought she had taken advantage of her? Would she take it to Nic's commander? But the kiss was instigated by Claire, not Nic. It wouldn't matter. Nic was an officer and she knew better. Nic needed answers from Claire before she did anything and she wanted them now.

Nic slammed the car in reverse and made her way to the highway. Thinking about everything that happened made Nic wonder who she was madder at, Claire or herself? She replayed the night in her head. She was sure Jordan had outed Claire in their conversation. Hadn't Jordan said that she was there with her friend who was going through some major stuff? Hadn't she said that Claire hadn't been around family, and then Jordan made the quotation marks when she said family, in a long time? Nic had more questions as she thought about the night's events, and she knew the only place to get those answers would be from Claire.

"Claire, pull over and let me drive."

Focusing on the road now was the least of Claire's worries. How could she not have noticed that it was Nic standing in front of Jordan? Claire let the car glide to a stop on the nearly deserted road. Turning to Jordan she tried to make sense of what had just happened, searching her friend's eyes for answers.

"What am I going to do, Jor? I can't believe that I just outed myself to Nic Caldwell. What is she going to think?" Claire scrubbed her face with her hands as she sat waiting for some wisdom from her friend.

"Look Claire, I know things seem bleak right now, but honestly, is this the worst thing that could happen? Think about it. Didn't you call me this week and tell me that you kissed her and that you thought you might have feelings for her?" Claire knew Jordan was trying to sound rational, but right now, she wasn't sure that was what she wanted to hear.

"Look, you and I both know that your marriage to Mike was like two kids who were playing house. It was great on the outside but inside, it wasn't real. You both never intended for it to last forever and unfortunately, it ended earlier than you anticipated. So now you get to move on to the next phase of your life." Jordan said, "Besides, look at the bright side. At least you know Ms. Gorgeous is gay. Right?"

Claire looked at the darkened road wishing she could change the events of the night. She felt as dark as the road ahead and knew that on some level Jordan was right. But Claire always worried about appearances-family appearances, military appearances and wifely appearances. She was an officer's wife, and she had learned early on that image was everything in the military, that it could make or break a spouse's career. But then again, Claire wouldn't have to worry about appearances for much longer now that Mike was gone. Turning, Claire could see that Jordan had that mischievous look on her face again.

Claire knew she was going to have a "come to Jesus" moment about being gay one day, she just didn't think it would be this soon and in this way. There was a lot to what Jordan was saying and she knew her friend was right. She had put her life on hold for over three years now, and the fact that she was in a position to be who she was scared her more than just a little.

CHAPTER NINETEEN

The warm day was sunny and inviting as Claire looked out the sliding glass door to the backyard. She sipped her coffee and stared out at nothing, thinking about the night before. How could she have been so stupid as to let Jordan talk her into going to a gay bar? Of all the stupid, idiotic things. Claire rested her head against the glass, feeling its cool slick imprint on her forehead and then it suddenly hit her.

"Nic is gay," Claire whispered. She became slightly giddy at the realization. "Nic is gay. Holy shit, Nic is gay!"

Claire stood back from the glass and focused on the beautiful day outside her window, not quite as scared as she had been last night. So her gaydar wasn't broken. She had suspected that something was different about Nic, but could never quite put her finger on it. Now she knew, Nic played for her team. Well, her old team. Claire hadn't been a team player for a very long time and now she was coming to the realization that she had a choice to make. She could continue with the charade of being a heterosexual or be who she really was, a lesbian with a beautiful daughter and a future full of possibilities.

Everything was happening very fast and Claire needed time to think. She needed to be by herself. She walked into the kitchen, poured another cup of coffee, and made her way to the guest bedroom. Peeking inside she could see Jordan spread across the queen-size bed.

"Jordan." Claire gently sat on the edge of the bed and set the coffees on the nightstand. "Jordie, sweetie, wake up."

"No."

"Aw come on, you can't be sleeping off a hangover cause you barely drank anything, remember?"

"I'm dreaming of a tall, sexy, green eyed woman who should be laying here naked next to me. But thanks to you, she'll never be mine," Jordan huffed as she pulled the covers over her head. "Now leave me alone you little home wrecker."

Claire started to giggle as she crawled under the covers with her friend. "Aw, come on Jor. You have me."

"It's not the same. I buy you dinner and you never put out, but Major Gorgeous, on the other hand, I bet she puts out. I can just imagine what she can put out," Jordan said as she peeked at Claire under the covers. "Besides, did you see her ass in those jeans? God, that woman should be shot for wearing her pants so tight with no underwear."

"Jordan, how do you know she wasn't wearing any underwear?" Claire wished she had paid closer attention to Nic, especially considering she occupied a lot of her thoughts lately. Claire vaguely remembered what Nic was wearing, and wasn't surprised in the least that Jordan had noticed the little detail of Nic's commando style. Jordan could undress a woman in less than two minutes, even if she was covered from head to toe in a ski-outfit. Claire had seen her do it to a cute little ski bunny when they were at a resort during college.

"God, I can't even imagine what would have happened if I hadn't come along," Claire said as she rested her head on Jordan's shoulder.

"Well, let's just say that you are occupying her place right now, sister. So maybe you can think of a way to make it up to me since I was in score mode before you rudely interrupted me." Turning towards Claire, Jordan slid her hand up and down her back and looked at her seductively.

"Whoa, there, cowgirl." Claire put her hands on Jordan's chest, forcing her back as Claire started to sit up. "Look, Romeo, you and I both know that there was no way you could have brought her back here. I live on base. Remember? If she got caught with a woman here she could lose her job."

"Hey, she's a big girl. She would have figured it out," Jordan said as she arched an eyebrow, "She does have a car with a backseat, right?"

"Jordan."

"I'm just kidding."

"I need some time to myself to think things through. I feel like I have too many balls in the air and if I'm not careful I'm going to drop them all. I just can't seem to focus on anything and I need to get out of here for a while. Do you mind watching Grace while I take the bike out?"

Claire knew she had to come to terms with her guilt over Mike's death, her sudden foray into lesbianism again, and her growing feelings for Nic. If she didn't, she would just turn and run and she didn't run away from things, she confronted them on her terms. She needed time to decide what to do next.

"Look, Jordan, if I don't do this I might have a meltdown. I don't want to make decisions about my life when I can't focus on anything longer than a few minutes. I'll be back before dinnertime. And I'll have my cell phone if you need anything. Please?"

"Hasn't it been a while since your rode your bike? I mean, are you sure it's all right to ride in the state you're in?" Jordan asked gently.

"I'll be fine. I just need some space right now, okay?" Claire said as she got off the bed and went to her room to change.

"Of course, honey. I'll watch Grace. Just be careful."

Nic woke up feeling pretty much like she had the night before. She was confused. Sleep hadn't cured her ills like she thought it would and she still had more questions than answers. The only person to give her those answers was Claire. Swinging her feet to the floor and stretching, she replayed the past couple of days over again to see if she missed something, anything, in her dealings with Claire.

Did Claire tell her she was gay and she missed it? Was she sending a signal that Nic didn't see? What was that comment Claire made about "how looks could be deceiving when it came to her and Mike"? Did she mean that she was really gay and that she was just using Mike? For what? What did Mike have that Claire couldn't get on her own? She was a college graduate, liberal studies with a teaching credential. So why was Claire married to Mike when she could clearly take care of herself? Did Mike know Claire was gay and if he did, how did he handle it? Fuck, Mike was a stand-up guy and he deserved better than that. Nic was getting mad now. How could Claire deceive him like that? And what about Grace?

Then there was the kiss. God that kiss. She felt her body stirring again, as she thought about how good Claire's lips tasted-sweet, hungry, and wanting. She wondered if Claire felt the same way after the kiss. Had she wanted more, like Nic did? Now Nic wasn't sure about anything.

Nic wondered how her life had turned so upside down. She hadn't felt this unsettled since the accident when no one would tell her what happened. She had barely started putting her life back in order and now it was all ass-backwards. Her emotions were raw and she was on edge. It wasn't so different from how she felt when she had come out to her parents. She rested her face against the cold tiles and let the hot water pummel her back as she remembered the first time she had fallen for another woman.

Nic needed to talk to Claire. She needed answers, because those answers were far more important than she had previously thought.

CHAPTER TWENTY

Nic arrived at Claire's and couldn't help but think how much her life had changed since their encounter. Meeting Claire had made her think about her life after the military. It had made her think about family and what she wanted out of life. She knew the life she really wanted would have to happen out of the military because what she wanted couldn't be while she was in. Claire had changed everything with a single... kiss.

Before Nic could knock on Claire's door, it swung open and the brunette from the previous night was standing before her, flashing that same seductive smile. Nic felt herself being cruised again.

"Well, Major Caldwell, you look absolutely edible in your leather outfit. I bet that gets you laid, doesn't it?" Jordan asked.

"It's Jordan, right? Look, Jordan, I need to talk to Claire. Can you tell her I'm here and would like to talk to her?" Nic said, feeling like she was the guest of honor at an all-you-can-eat lesbian buffet.

"No."

"What do you mean no? Look, I know you're her friend and all, and I am sure you want to protect her but I'm not the enemy, trust me."

"Listen Major, the reason I was at the door so quickly was because I thought you were Claire. She took off a few hours ago on her bike and forgot her cell phone. She isn't back yet so I've been a little worried about her."

"Did she say where she was going or when she would be back?"

"No, she just said she needed some space and time. Typical Claire."

"Well why don't I go out and see if I can find her? Did you see which way she went?"

Jordan pointed. "She did say something about the back roads on post being peaceful and relaxing."

"Well that's a start." It was a statement more than a question as Nic assumed control of the situation. "Can I ask you a question?"

"Depends. Are you asking me out?" Jordan asked jokingly.

"Doubtful. You are persistent though, aren't you?" Nic chuckled. She knew she should be flattered but she didn't want to lead Jordan on in any way. Her focus was Claire and the more she thought about it, the more she knew that her focus would always be Claire.

"What do you wanna know?"

"You don't have to answer if you don't want, but how long have you known Claire?"

"Since college. Why?"

"Well… Did you mean what you said last night about your friend being gay?"

"Nic, are you asking me if Claire is a lesbian?"

"Yes, I guess I am."

"Look, what I said last night wasn't a lie, but I was there for me, not Claire. She was just along for the ride. I thought she could do with a change of scenery, so I got her out of the house."

"Are you two involved?" Nic asked, hoping that she hadn't just crossed a line.

Jordan stayed silent for so long Nic began to wonder if she was going to receive an answer at all. She watched as various emotions ran through Jordan's eyes. "No, we aren't involved. She's my best friend. But let me say this, Major Caldwell," she continued, taking a step closer to Nic, "If anyone hurts my friend, they would have to deal with me and trust me, you don't want to deal with me when I am pissed."

"Well, I guess I'd better get going and see if I can find Claire. Thanks, Jordan. I appreciate your candor. Just for the record, I don't want to see Claire get hurt either." Turning, Nic felt Jordan's eye burning a hole right through her as she walked back to her bike.

CHAPTER TWENTY-ONE

Claire sat on the side of the road, chastising herself for not looking at the gas gauge before leaving. She had left the house so fast that she had forgotten her cell phone, and now she was stuck out in the middle of nowhere with no cell phone and no way of getting help. She had been there for forty-five minutes without a single car passing by. She took her jacket off and slung it over the seat of her bike and wiped her face off with her head rag. It was hot out in the back country and she definitely had not prepared to be stranded. She didn't have water, a snack, or anything that would keep her hydrated for a long wait outside. Ten more minutes and she would walk for help. She'd just have to hope that no one would bother her bike if she left it alone for a while.

She had wanted time and space to think, and that was all she had done for the past two hours. She had thought about Mike and Grace, but mostly she had thought about last night and Nic. As long as the possibility of Nic being straight was out there, she could kid herself that Nic wasn't an option in her life. In all actuality, though, the Major *wasn't* an option and Claire knew it. Nic was a Marine and, unless the military had changed its policy in the past ten hours, Nic was not about to give up her career for Claire, and Claire wasn't about to ask her to do that on a "maybe" while they got to know each other better. Claire knew Nic's type-they bled camouflage when wounded. Duty, honor, and country before everything else. Nic had a duty to do and Claire was just a duty as far as Nic was concerned.

Claire remembered the kiss they had shared in the bathroom. That had nothing to do with duty, did it? Why had Nic kissed her? If she was honest with herself, she had kissed Nic, not the other way around. Nevertheless, Nic kissed her back. She could still feel Nic's hands buried in her hair, pulling her closer. Claire's core clenched as she thought about that kiss, about seeing Nic naked, well almost naked, and how gorgeous she was. Claire had thought about Nic a lot when she was finally alone at night. That was dangerous territory to explore and Claire knew it. She found herself attracted to Nic and wouldn't deny it. She was everything Mike was and more. She spoke about a future outside the Corps, something Mike had never done. She made Claire weak when she was around, and that was something Mike had never done either.

Now Claire wondered why she had ever married Mike. Had she reacted too quickly to his promise of family, travel and stability? Couldn't she have had that with a woman? Claire found herself questioning every decision she had made since college, and now she had an opportunity to make a change that she could live with. She didn't need her father's approval any longer. She could change her life so that she and Grace would be happy, and stop moving from base to base, waiting for that next rank. She could only have had a truly stable life if she had left Mike.

She winced and kicked at the loose sand around her feet. Part of that decision had been made for her. She wiped away a tear as it made its way down her cheek.

Was it fair for Grace to grow up in a lesbian relationship? *Why not?* She had grown up in what amounted to a single parent household with a caring, but absentee father. Grace was ahead of the game. She had a mother who adored her, and that was all that really mattered.

What would she do after the funeral was over, when everyone went home and it was just her and Grace? She needed to think about her future. What she would do for work, and where they would live. She liked California, and if she was going to finally accept who she was, she could think of worse places to live while raising a daughter. She had requested an extension to stay in housing when the Corps had lost Mike's body so she had 30 days after that time to leave. That would give her some time to find a place and look for a job, something she had been putting off in the face of all the chaos.

Well, tomorrow was as good a time as any to get started on that task and start boxing things up in the house. She sighed in frustration; her new resolve sparking a desire to get her life started. She had so much to do, and here she was stranded on the side of the road waiting for any Good Samaritan to stop by and lend a hand. Claire looked down the road seeing an object getting closer to her. She stood up, ready to finally wave down the motorist.

CHAPTER TWENTY-TWO

Nic was just about ready to give up and call the M.P.'s when she decided to turn down the last road she could think of. Making a right, she noticed something about half a mile down the road and sighed in relief to finally have found Claire. She was worried sick that Claire had crashed and she was in a hospital somewhere, or worse, that she had met someone who had made an offer of help and instead kidnapped her. Not that it was in any way likely on base, but Nic couldn't believe how irrational her thought processes had become since meeting Claire. Kissing her in the bathroom, dreaming about her at night, seeing her in a gay bar, and now panicking about her impending demise at the hands of an unknown assailant. *Get a grip. She's fine.* Nic eased her grip on the handlebars, her white knuckles finally getting some blood flow now that she had found Claire safe and sound.

"Hey stranger," Nic said, the relief evident in her voice as she pulled her bike in behind Claire's, trying to focus on Claire's face rather than how fucking incredible she looked in her motorcycle clothes.

"Gosh, am I glad to see you. It seems that I've forgotten my phone and I ran out of gas. Stupid, huh?" Claire looked at Nic's broad smile, wishing she could kiss those sexy, full lips.

"Naw, it's happened to me before. I'm just glad I finally found you. I've been looking all over post. I was getting ready to call out the dogs." Laughing, Nic pulled off her gloves and helmet and set them on the tank, resting her hands on top of the helmet. "So, how long have you been out here?"

"About forty-five minutes. I thought about pushing the bike but I wouldn't have gotten very far. It's pretty heavy, and the heat would have gotten the better of me so I was waiting for a Good Samaritan to come by and save me. Lucky for me, you happen to be that Good Samaritan."

Nic swung off her bike and walked over to Claire's Harley, hoping she was right and that Claire really was flirting with her. She circled the cold machine. She held out her hand. "Keys?"

Claire handed the keys to her bike and watched as Nic took the gas cap off the top of the tank, peering inside the empty vessel.

"Looks like you're dry, but it could be something else. Did you turn the petcock so that it hit the reserve?"

"Of course Nic. I'm not stupid," Claire said in a huff. She immediately held her hands up apologetically. "Sorry, I guess the heat is getting to me. I turned it about 5 minutes before it quit. I thought I had more time." She regretted her tough tone immediately when she saw Nic's face fall.

"No harm, no foul." Nic looked down at the engine trying to hide her disappointment at Claire's sudden anger.

"Well, why don't we call a tow truck just to make sure that everything is all right. Better to be safe than risk anything. Right?" Nic hoped Claire would agree with her reasoning. She wanted to make sure that it was only an empty gas tank and not something more serious. She wouldn't forgive herself if Claire got hurt due to an oversight on her part.

"Do you really think that's necessary?"

"I do. I just want to make sure and have it checked out. But if you want to ride it back, I'll go get some gas."

"No, you're probably right. Better safe than sorry. I guess that means you'll need to give me a ride back." She smiled at the thought of riding behind Nic.

"Well, if you insist. I mean you could walk back if you want. I don't want to assume anything." Nic could see the shocked look on Claire's face at the thought of walking all the way back to her house.

"Cute, smarty pants. I think I'll just take the offer of a ride back. I can trust you, can't I?" Claire let the innuendo hang out there as she spoke again, "I mean it's probably been a while since you rode two-up, hasn't it?" Claire could banter with the best of them and she knew Nic was definitely able to give her a ride back. She liked the way Nic's eyes sparkled in the mid day light, lighting up her smile and creating a glow around her.

"I think I can handle you any time lady. Just wait and see." Nic said, letting her own innuendo hang in the same sexually charged air between them.

"I guess we'll see."

"I'll call and get a truck on its way and then you can call Jordan and let her know you're okay."

"Good idea."

Nic made the arrangements to have Claire's bike picked up by a special tow truck for motorcycles. Claire then called Jordan to let her know that Nic had found her and that they would be home shortly. Nic smiled as Claire laughed at something Grace was saying to her mom.

From the gist of the conversation with Grace, she could hear that Auntie Jordan was taking Grace to the beach for the afternoon to make sand castles. What a break for Nic. They wouldn't have to be in a hurry to get home so maybe they could talk after all. As she watched Claire talk and laugh on the phone, she thought about how she was going to broach the subject of last night with Claire. She thought her best bet would be to come right out and ask, but she wasn't sure how Claire would respond to the direct approach. Would she be defensive? *What if she doesn't want to talk about it?* She didn't want to scare Claire off. Claire closed the phone and handed it back to Nic.

"So, Nic, you're a lesbian?" Claire chuckled at the shocked look on Nic's face.

"Well, I guess you're a lesbian too, huh? I mean, you were in a gay bar last night too." Nic knew she sounded like a petulant child and she winced.

"Hey, don't try to change the subject here, this is about you not me."

"What?"

"You heard me. This is about you. I was there with my friend, but you were alone. Right?"

"Wait, wait just a minute. Are you denying you're a lesbian? Before you answer that, let me say that Jordan has already pretty much outed you without knowing it." Nic said. "So let's try this again." She held out her hand.

"Hi. I'm Nic and I am a lesbian." Nic flashed Claire a smile that made her want to drop to her knees and thank god for miracles.

The tingle that shot through Claire as she grabbed Nic's hand went right to her clit. She briefly closed her eyes and reveled in the warm grasp. She stopped herself before she let out a moan at Nic's touch.

"So Claire, do you have something you want to tell me?" Nic asked seductively as she stepped closer.

Claire was looking directly at Nic's chest, having a hard time looking her in the eye, unable to form the words that needed to come out. She could feel her heart start to beat faster at their contact and knew she was doomed as her body responded. She could feel Nic's warm breath on her neck and turned so her lips grazed Nic's. She pulled Nic in closer and kissed her. Her lips felt as if they were on fire.

A soft moan slipped from Claire as she started to move her hips against Nic's thigh, her body betraying her at every level and Claire knew there was no going back. She slowly opened her mouth as Nic's tongue searched for entry, deepening their contact further. She felt Nic's mouth move from hers to travel along her chin and down to her neck where Nic's kisses left searing patches of desire. She pulled Nic closer to her body and began to slide up and down the long leg that had wedged itself between her thighs.

Claire threw her head back as Nic continued down towards her chest. "Fuck," slipped from Claire's lips as she felt the sexual heat roll off Nic's body.

"Nic, please. We need to stop. Please. What if someone drives by and sees us?"

Nic could hardly hear Claire over the blood pounding in her ears. Her whole body flushed as she made her way down the soft skin of Claire's chest. Her hands moved to the front of Claire's chest, palming her breasts, lifting them and rubbing her thumbs over the erect nipples that begged to be released from their confines.

"Nic," whispered Claire, desperate for more contact

but scared that someone would drive by and see the enamored couple.

As if someone had splashed cold water on her, Nic stepped back and rubbed her hands down her jeans, trying to replace the touch of Claire's breast with a different kind of friction. "God, Claire, I'm sorry. I don't know what came over me. I'm —"

"Nic, stop." Stepping closer to Nic, Claire ran her hand along Nic's face looking into her confused eyes.

"Nic, I wanted that just as much as you did. I guess that answers your question, doesn't it?"

"Yeah, I guess it does, but I'm not sure if that's a good thing."

"What? What do you mean? I thought you would be relieved, I mean well...I don't know what I mean." Claire felt a pang of panic at the thought that Nic might not want something with her after all.

"Claire, I think we need to talk."

"What do you want to know?"

"Everything you want to tell me."

Claire told Nic about her own loss when she was slightly older than Grace. She could barely remember her mother anymore, now that she thought about it.

"I remember the day my mom died. My dad was waiting with my grandma for me when I got home from school."

It was seared into her brain like a brand that could never be removed. Her father was never one for mincing words so he was about to blurt it out when Claire's grandmother took her by the hand and led her to Claire's bedroom to explain a loss that would forever change her life.

"I'm so sorry, Claire," Nic wrapped her arms around Claire and held her tight. Claire told Nic about how her father treated her growing up and Nic thought about how similar their fathers were.

Claire explained how she felt with no mother in the house, explaining how she never had that maternal touch that so many of her friends had growing up.

"My dad was demanding, and he never let me forget it. When we had dinner he would drill into my head what was expected from me. And then it all came crashing down when I was in high school." Claire looked up into Nic's understanding eyes. There was no judgment in her gaze, just understanding. Nic held her tighter.

"I told him about this girl I had a crush on. That was it. I had committed the ultimate sin as far as he was concerned."

"Oh Claire, I'm so sorry," Nic said as she kissed the top of Claire's head. "I wish you didn't have to go through all of that."

"It's okay, Nic," Claire said nonchalantly. "Basically, it's made me the person I am today."

Claire shook her head as if she was trying to physically release herself from the bad memories. Why she would remember all of this now, when she had worked so hard to forget it, only reminded Claire that her father still influenced her. Claire had to tell herself that Grace was her only focus right now and that was all that mattered.

Claire explained how shocked she had been when she found out that she had gotten pregnant.

"It was the one and only time Mike and I had sex. We had been drinking, I got emotional and the next thing I knew we were making love. Nine months later Grace was born."

"Some men have all the luck," Nic said stroking Claire's hair.

"Interestingly, that's kinda how Mike felt. He convinced me to keep Grace, offering to take care of both of us if I married him. I knew it would give him the respectability he needed to stay in the military." Claire took a long deep breath and let it out slowly.

"What do you mean?"

"He was gay, Nic. Didn't you know? No you probably didn't. He was very discrete."

It took a minute for it to sink in before Nic could say anything.

"Wait, let me get this straight, no pun intended. Mike was gay?"

"Yep"

"No shit." Nic couldn't hide the shocked look on her face. "I can't believe it. He had it all, a wife, a beautiful little girl and his career. Fuck!"

By the time the tow truck arrived, twenty minutes later, Claire had told Nic almost everything. She even talked about the last relationship she had with a woman in college. There was always talk amongst the troops about who was thought to be gay and who wasn't, but Mike's name never came up. Claire explained that she and Mike had already discussed divorce and that the time he spent away from Grace was making it easier to make that happen. Mike was focused more on his career and had told Claire that he would probably do another overseas tour so that he could move more quickly up the ranks. Grace was important to him, but he made it clear that his career was very important and he would do what he had to do to advance.

Nic felt that she had a good picture of Claire and Mike's relationship, but that wasn't to say she wasn't surprised at the revelations Claire presented to her.

Nic noticed the driver motion to them; informing Claire he was ready to take the bike to a nearby shop. Claire briefly spoke with the driver and then was by Nic's side, putting on her jacket and helmet.

"Ready?"

Nic nodded and held out a hand to assist Claire on to the back of her bike.

"If I go too fast just let me know."

"I think I can handle a little speed, Major."

"I'm sure you can but just in case, just squeeze me and I'll slow down," Nic said smirking. "Sorry I don't have a back rest. I rarely have passengers so I took it off. Besides, I think it makes the bike look hotter."

"I think it's the driver that makes the bike look hot." Claire found that flirting with Nic had some perks that she hoped she could take advantage of at a later time.

"Oh shoot. I forgot my gloves in the bike." Claire knew it was too late as she watched the tow truck turn the corner.

"Well, you can put your hands in my jacket pockets if they get cold." Nic's eyes twinkled at the thought of Claire's hands wrapped around her body.

"I don't think that will be necessary, do you? I mean, it is still nice out."

"You're probably right." Nic said as she swung her leg over the bike and put the kickstand up. Nic started the motorcycle and felt Claire settle behind her. The positioning of the back seat put the v of Claire's legs right against Nic's lower back and the contact sent a surge of energy coursing through Nic's body. She reached her left hand over and caressed the leather-clad thigh that had settled nicely against her.

"Ready?"

"Yep, let's ride."

Nic pulled the bike onto the pavement and goosed the throttle just enough, causing Claire to grab her quickly around her chest. Without realizing it, Claire grabbed Nic's breasts and held tight as Nic added more throttle to the pavement.

"Hey smarty, careful there, I want to make it home in one piece," Claire shouted into Nic's ear.

"I gotcha covered, don't worry."

Nic felt Claire adjust her position on the bike and lean into Nic's back. The contact was making it hard for Nic to focus on the road instead, she focused on the leather-clad breasts pressing against her. Rolling down the back roads of the base, she thought about how good it felt to ride two-up with Claire. The feel of the body pressing against hers, the way Claire's legs were hugging her and the warm breath on the back of her neck made Nic's body tighter with each mile they went. Suddenly, Nic felt Claire's hands reach under her jacket and grab her waist.

"Sorry. I guess my hands are cold after all." The contact caused Nic's abs to tighten and she felt her breathing pick up. It was going to be a long ride back to Claire's and she didn't know how she was going to be able to concentrate with Claire touching her body. It was one thing to have leather separating them, but another when that buffer was gone and the contact was almost skin on skin.

"No problem. It can be pretty chilly in the afternoon around here." Nic turned her head towards Claire's so Claire could hear her over the engine and wind. Claire's lips were only a few inches away and it was all Nic could do not to try and kiss them before turning back and focusing on the road ahead. Nic wondered if Claire knew what she was doing to her.

Claire rested her head on Nic's shoulder and without realizing what she was doing; she started to caress the hard abs under her hands. She continued reaching around and gently squeezed Nic's body. Closing her eyes, she allowed the vibration of the motorcycle to rub her against the strong body in front of her, her clit hardening at the contact. She could smell Nic's perfume and its calming effects sent a surge through her body. Slowly she worked her hands in different directions on Nic's body. One started a slow migration to the firm breast under Nic's T-shirt, the other made a small circular pattern across Nic's abs venturing lower down.

Claire continued her gentle caresses and felt something on Nic's lower abs, a belly button ring. Claire smiled at the discovery and wondered why she had never noticed the jewelry before now. Probably because she was always focused on other parts of Nic's anatomy, like her breasts, her long muscular legs, or her seductively gorgeous face that sent her head swimming every time she looked at Nic. Claire marveled at the hard body she was caressing.

It had been a long time since she had touched a woman this intimately and she was glad she hadn't forgotten how much she enjoyed the close maneuvers. She wondered what Nic's naked body would feel like against her own. Her sculpted, powerful muscles holding Claire's body down and her own body rocking against those powerful thighs that kept them seated securely on the bike. Claire nearly moaned as she thought how powerful Nic looked sheathed in her leather chaps and vest. Nic was the type of woman every lesbian dreamed about. Strong, caring, chivalrous, and drop dead sexy.

"Do you know how many fantasies I have had about you, Nic," Claire whispered in Nic's ear.

"No, why don't you tell me?" Nic turned slightly, smiling as she said it.

"Which one? The one where I tie you to the bed and have my way with your sexy body?" Claire felt Nic's body tighten slightly as she whispered in her ear again. "Or the one where you take me for a ride on your motorcycle and we...." Claire purposely let the sentence hang out there.

"Yes?" Nic said as a tingle went right through her to her vibrating clit.

"How about you? Ever fantasize?" Claire wondered if the fantasy would live up to the real thing in bed. How did Nic make love? Was she gentle or hard? Did she like to take control or give control to her lover, begging for release? Claire felt a blush roll up her neck to her face, glad Nic couldn't see her illicit thoughts showing themselves so blatantly.

Claire could feel herself getting wet and knew she was definitely in trouble if she kept these thoughts going. She wanted Nic in a bad way. It scared her as she thought about what would happen when this was all over. What would she do if she gave in to her desires to make love to Nic? What would Nic do if Claire threw herself at her? Turn her down, walk away or take what Claire was offering her? That was a whole other question wasn't it? What was Claire offering her, a woman with a child? A life outside of the military? What? Nic had a lot to lose if she was found out to be a lesbian. Claire knew that what she was offering wasn't fair to Nic. Laying her head on Nic's back, Claire stopped moving her hands and gently laid them on Nic's hips. What was she thinking caressing Nic like she was her lover?

CHAPTER TWENTY-THREE

Nic coasted to the stoplight and put her feet on the pavement as she steadied the bike underneath them. Without thinking, she covered Claire's hands and pulled them around her body, hugging herself with the strong arms that had encircled her earlier. As much as she had enjoyed it, she was glad Claire had stopped caressing her so skillfully. It killed her concentration and she could have dumped the bike the way her hands were shaking. She held tightly to Claire's hands and leaned back against her, waiting for the light to change.

Nic heard Claire whisper in her ear, "Sorry about earlier. I don't know what I was thinking."

"Don't apologize. I liked it."

Grabbing Claire's hands she gently brought them up to her breasts and pressed them against her hardened nipples.

"Does that feel like I'm experiencing a hardship here?"

"No, I guess not. I just didn't want you to think I was taking advantage of the situation." Claire gently pressed Nic's hard nipples between her fingers, smiling when Nic tensed and pushed against her hands.

"Please take advantage of me all you want. I enjoy being taken advantage of by a beautiful woman but, I have to warn you, I can't be held responsible for my actions if you continue." Nic's smirk and lusty look spoke volumes to Claire and she found herself responding to the innuendo, allowing a flare of hope to develop beneath the heat of desire already flaring.

"Well maybe I don't want you to be responsible this once."

"Careful. You're playing with fire."

"Maybe I know how to put out that kind of fire, or maybe I would rather stoke it. Guess that depends on you." Claire lowered her eyes to Nic's lips. "Maybe you should get me home. I don't know about you, but I'm feeling rather heated and need to get out of this leather."

Nic pulled the bike back onto the road and gunned the motorcycle once again. This time she didn't slow down and felt Claire grab her breasts once again. Five minutes later, Nic pulled her Yamaha into Claire's driveway and dropped the kickstand down onto the cement. Nic swung off her bike and extended her hand to help Claire off the bike. Nic felt her body tighten as Claire grabbed her hand and pulled her towards the quarters. Nic looked around to see if anyone was watching, and felt herself pulled into the house without a backwards glance from Claire.

"Claire…"

"Shh." Claire covered Nic's lips with a finger and pulled her in the direction of her bedroom. "Nothing Nic, say nothing please unless you don't want this. Then you can say something."

Nic looked at Claire and shook her head slowly. She had thought about this, dreamed about this and now here she was in Claire's bedroom watching as Claire shed her jacket.

"Sit." Nic felt Claire push her backwards onto the bed.

"Watch." Claire peeled her damp T-shirt over her head.

Nic had a view of both the front and the back as she watched Claire in the full-length mirrored closet doors. Nic let go of the breath she was holding as Claire moved closer. She felt her body shudder as a tingle coursed through her. She had to control her hands, when all she wanted to do was pull Claire to her and make love to her. Claire turned and faced the mirrors presenting her back to Nic.

"Please."

"Oh, God. You have no idea how long I've thought about this moment," Nic said as she raised shaking hands to Claire's sexy body.

Nic undid the floral bra and watched it slide to the floor, hoping that Claire had on matching panties under her leather pants. She was a sucker for silky lace underwear that matched. Fetish? Maybe, but it was sexy as hell when a woman took the time to make sure that her underwear was just as important as her outer appearance. Nic watched Claire's face in the mirror as Claire backed up towards her companion, swaying her hips seductively. Standing, Nic stepped closer to Claire's naked back, pulling Claire toward her tingling body. Nic's lips tenderly caressed Claire's neck, her hands gently glided down Claire's soft arms and then around to her front and caressed her breasts. She looked up to see Claire watching in the mirror as she pulled and tugged on her nipples. Nic could feel her clit tightening at the erotic scene playing out in front of her, watching and being watched.

She rubbed herself against Claire's hard ass as she ran one of her hands down into the tight leather pants Claire had on. Nic watched as Claire reached down and undid the snap and zipper, slowly opening the front for easier access. Nic cupped Claire's clit and slid a finger slowly down further into the wetness between Claire's legs. She heard Claire gasp when she barely touched her opening.

"Nic, let me take these off."

"I'll do it. You just stand there and let me do all the work." She slid down Claire's back, kissing her as she went down behind the beautiful body. She reached down and pulled Claire's boots and socks off and tossed them across the room. She didn't want anything in her way when she finally had Claire's body all to herself. She watched in the mirror as she slid Claire's leather pants down slowly, exposing her nakedness. No panties. Nic helped Claire step out of her pants and tossed them in the direction of the boots.

"Don't move. I just want to look at your beautifully sculpted body. God you're gorgeous, Claire. I hope that doesn't sound like I'm just saying that to get into your pants?" Chuckling at the silliness of the statement, Nic slowly rose behind Claire, rubbing her clothed body gently against Claire's naked body, reaching around and running her hands up and down Claire's legs. Closing her eyes she felt Claire's body relax into her touch, giving herself to Nic.

"Nic?" Claire said in a soft, husky voice.

"Yeah?" Nic could barely mouth the words as she caressed Claire softly.

Nic watched as Claire turned and grabbed her hand and pulled her in the direction of the bathroom.

"Shower! I want everything to be perfect for our

first time." Claire looked at Nic seductively, licking her lips. "Is that okay?"

"How can I say no?" Nic let herself be pulled into the bathroom.

Pulling the shower curtain back, Claire started the shower.

"Now it's my turn to undress you," Claire said, reaching for Nic.

Nic couldn't take her eyes off of Claire's body as she started unbuttoning her shirt. Slowly Claire pulled the shirt down Nic's arm. Stopping the shirt midway, she pulled Nic towards her and reached up for a kiss. Nic was trapped and she knew it. Claire could do anything to her and she would not be able to resist.

"You taste good," Claire whispered against Nic's lips. "I wonder how the rest of you is gonna taste."

Nic felt her heart racing as Claire pulled her in for another kiss.

"Hmm, really good."

Going back to her task, Claire dropped Nic's shirt to the floor and rubbed her hands up Nic's muscular arms.

"Fuck, you're killing me," Nic said, moaning.

"Really? I can stop if you want me to."

"Don't you dare."

Slowly Claire walked around Nic, her hand trailing along Nic's body. Claire could see the vein in Nic's neck pulsing quicker as she made her way around to the front of Nic. Claire palmed Nic's firm breasts before she seductively let her tongue make a trail around one of her nipples. Slowly, she traveled to the other one and gently played with it, working the nipple with her tongue. Claire felt Nic's hands gently grip both sides of her face.

"Claire, if you don't stop you're gonna make me come. Please have some mercy."

Claire looked up from what she had been doing and smiled.

"And that would be a bad thing?"

It had been a long time since Claire had seduced anyone and it was nice to know she still had the touch. Kissing Nic again Claire started working on Nic's chaps, letting them drop to the floor after unzipping them, and then removed her boots and socks. The room was starting to mist up from the heat of the shower and Claire knew she was getting wet from the anticipation. Biting her lip, she peeled Nic's pants down her long legs.

Finally, thought Nic. Never had she been undressed so seductively, and it was killing her. Pulling Claire to her feet Nic grabbed Claire's hand and slid it into her panties.

"See what you're doing to me," Nic whispered into Claire's ear.

Nic watched as Claire slowly rubbed her clit back and forth causing her to moan. A gasp escaped Nic's lips as Claire slid a finger inside her and moved it in and out of her wet pussy.

"Claire," Nic could barely talk as she tried to control the orgasm that started to take hold of her. Covering Claire's hand, Nic started to buck against it as her body responded instantly to the stroking.

"Fuck, I'm gonna come Claire, shit." Nic felt herself tighten around Claire's finger as Claire bent down and gently bit Nic's nipple. "Oh god."

Nic bucked harder as she pushed Claire's hand tighter into her clit.

"Oh baby," was all Nic could say as she came.

Nic was breathing hard as she pulled Claire tighter

into her and kissed her. Nic started to grind her hips into Claire as another orgasm coursed through her. Nic threw her head back and grunted as she felt her body release again.

Claire pulled Nic close as her body gently convulsed through the orgasm. It excited her to watch a woman come again, but this wasn't just any woman. It was Nic.

"God, that was hot baby. You ready for that shower now?" Claire watched as Nic's eyes closed and then slowly opened again looking like she was going to devour her.

"You're bad. Really bad, you know that?" Nic said as she grabbed Claire's hand and pulled her into the shower.

"If truth be told, I surprised myself," Claire said as she ducked into the fine spray.

She watched as Nic flung her panties on the pile of clothes and stepped into the spray with her. Reaching for the soap Claire lathered up her hands and immediately put them on Nic's breasts, feeling her nipples harden under her palms. Gently she washed Nic's breasts as she stared into Nic's half closed eyes. Nic looked like she was in a trance and barely moved, one hand on each of Claire's hips.

"You're killin' me you know,"

"Yeah? But what a way to go."

Nic's body shuddered again as Claire's hand dropped down between Nic's legs. Slowly she caressed Nic again, watching as Nic closed her eyes and dropped her head on Claire's shoulder. Claire heard Nic suck in a breath as she worked her clit again.

"Careful with that soap," Nic said as she kissed Claire's neck.

"Don't worry. I'll make sure I rinse before I fuck you again."

Claire felt both her hands grabbed and held.

"I think it's your turn," Nic said as she slowly moved Claire's hands behind her. Claire's nipples became the focus of Nic's attention as she moved between them, licking, biting and sucking. Nic slowly moved up Claire's chest kissing her neck again. This time she gently bit her neck as she kissed it, sending tingles through Claire. Nic's slick body gently slid up and down Claire's causing Claire's nipples to harden even more.

"Oh god Nic, please?"

"Hmm, what's wrong baby? Too much for you?" Nic smiled. "Tell you what - why don't we finish in here and we can really finish what we started out there."

Claire swallowed hard, "Now that sounds like a plan."

Nic grabbed the soap and handed it to Claire, "Ladies first."

Claire started to reach for Nic. "Nope, finish washing up I mean."

CHAPTER TWENTY-FOUR

Nic wrapped a towel around herself and watched as Claire dried off. Grabbing Claire's hand she walked to the side of the bed and sat down pulling Claire into her lap.

Nic could feel her own body reacting to the vision in front of her as she stroked a breast with one hand and slid her other up to Claire's neck. She slowly caressed the offered neck that lay bare before her. She heard Claire gasp as she made contact with a sensitive spot on her neck, causing Nic's clit to throb.

"Oh God, Nic, I want to feel you inside me, please..." Claire slid her hand up to Nic's hand and pulled it to her lips. Taking Nic's index finger, she seductively slid it into her mouth and sucked on the tip. She slid another finger past her lips to join the other, her tongue caressed the two fingers. Slowly pulling them back out, she slid Nic's hand down to her clit and began stroking herself with Nic's hand. Her nipples hardened even more as she watched Nic's hand dance across her clit. Each pass sent a jolt of pleasure throughout her body.

"Nic, please. I don't think I can stand much longer, I need you to...."

Nic's knees gently spread her legs open, exposing her fully. Claire bit her lower lip as she watched Nic caressing her inner thigh with one hand and her clit with the other. She met Nic's half lidded gaze in their reflection and licked her lips as she grabbed Nic's other hand and began sucking on two more fingers.

Wetting them, she slid them down. "Nic I want to feel you inside me. I need to come." She closed her eyes and whimpered as Nic slid her fingers along the outside of her swollen, wet labia. "Please."

"Are you sure? There's no going back after this baby." Nic's seductive stare reflected the same need that showed in Claire's eyes.

"Nic, please fuck me before I have to do it myself."

Nic arched an eyebrow. "Now that is something I'd like to see."

"Right now? If you don't do something quick you're not going to leave me with any alternative but to take care of business myself." Seductively, Claire covered Nic's hand with her own and started to stroke her clit.

"I don't want to leave a woman in distress. Besides, we have plenty of time for that later if you're a good girl." Grinning, Nic began to stroke her lover's hard clit. She watched as Claire laid her head back on her shoulder and started to grind her hips against Nic's hand. Every time she stroked the tender area, she felt Claire jerk and moan sending spasms through Nic's clit as Claire's ass rubbed against her.

Nic's tongue slid along Claire's earlobe and down her neck sending goose bumps down Claire's arms. Nic could feel the muscles in her arm flex as she stroked Claire. Her strong arms wrapped around Claire as she thought about every dream she was about to fulfill. Strength, power and control were her calling card yet she knew she wasn't the one in control, not this time. She focused on Claire's pleasure with each stroke of fingers across her clit. Nic slipped a finger on each side of Claire's clit and began a circular motion nestling her fingers between Claire's outer lips. Nic could barely remember to breathe as she watched Claire's tongue trail sensuously across her lips and moan again with pleasure.

"Baby, I want you to reach up and squeeze your nipples for me. Can you do that?" Nic watched as Claire did exactly as she was asked, pulling and tugging on the rosey areolas. Nic knew she wasn't going to last much longer if she continued to watch the erotic show in the mirror so she lowered her head and continued to kiss Claire's soft neck. *Focus, Focus, Focus, or you're a goner, Caldwell.*

Nic sucked in a breath and looked up as she heard Claire whisper, "Is that what you want baby?" while pulling her nipples harder for Nic.

"Oh fuck."

"Oh, baby" Claire reached down and grabbed Nic's hand forcing it deeper into her. Claire's tight vagina pulled Nic's fingers deeper as she stroked harder. "Oh fuck me baby, please, I need to come, please make me come."

Nic felt Claire grab her hand and rock it back and forth inside her, each stroke deeper than the last. She knew Claire was close but then so was she, the reflection in the mirror adding more fuel to the already out of control fire that raged through Nic. The more she watched, the wetter she was getting. She wouldn't last and knew she was going to come at any moment. Claire's muscles started to spasm on Nic as she felt her own orgasm start. Claire jerked on Nic's lap pumping furiously into Nic's hand as her ass jerked across Nic's clit. Nic's body tightened and jerked causing her to pull Claire's orgasming body into hers. They both arched at the same time as their orgasms ripped through them.

Nic started to slip her hand free from its warm shell but Claire stopped her. "Please, don't." Holding Nic's hand to her clit, Claire could still feel the tremors jerk through her. "I'm gonna come again, please." Claire pulled Nic's hand up and licked herself off Nic's hand rewetting Nic's fingers again. Sliding the hand across her clit she felt herself harden again at the contact. Claire reached up and began playing with a nipple as she whispered in Nic's ear.

"Fuck me again, baby."

Nic watched in the mirror as Claire stroked and rubbed her own nipple and Nic felt Claire's clit distend against her fingertips. She had never been with someone who could come again so quickly and she found herself grinding against Claire's ass at the request for more. Just when Nic thought she couldn't take any more, Claire reached up and ran her hands through Nic's hair grabbing her head as she slid her hips back and forth across Nic.

"Oh that's it baby, right there, right there. Fuck."

Nic started to slide her fingers in and out of the tight muscles, almost not able to move them, but she felt her hand stopped before she took another stroke.

"You don't have to fuck me, baby, just leave it in there, deep. I love the way you feel inside me. Just stay there." Claire stopped the motion of Nic's hand as Nic watched Claire reach up and grab her other nipple, torturing it in the same fashion she had the other. Claire closed her eyes and laid her head back on Nic's shoulder as she felt her body start to tremble again with the start of another orgasm. It had been a long time since she had been intimate like this and she wasn't sure if she would be able to come, but Nic's touch was amazing and her body reacted quickly to it. She could hear Nic's heavy breathing in her ear, and it only helped to spur her on more quickly as her body jerked back and forth over Nic's lap.

She heard Nic whisper in her ear "That's it baby. Come for me That's it. God, you're beautiful when you come. Fuck, you make me wet watching you like this."

That was all it took for Claire to explode on Nic's lap, spasming and jerking as she came in Nic's hand. Nic kept whispering in her ear as she stiffened and arched into Nic, her body out of control as she came again. Claire exhaled the breath she had been holding, and felt as if she was dissolving into a puddle, losing all control of herself.

Nic lowered their bodies down onto the bed, Claire still on top of Nic. With her hands between Claire's legs, Nic closed her eyes and remembered the sight of Claire's legs wide open with her hands between them, fucking her hard. Nic felt herself tighten with the memory and rolled herself and Claire onto their sides, slowly removing her hand from inside of Claire. Cradling Claire's petite body, Nic wrapped herself around her as if she was protecting her from some unknown evil.

Nic softly kissed the silken shoulder in front of her, tasting soap from their shower and sweat from their lovemaking. Nic shuddered and exhaled, contentment finding a home inside her head and heart. Making love to Claire was more than she could have dreamed. Her fantasies didn't even come close to what had just happened. She wanted to lay there forever and not return to the real world. She wanted to stay just like this. She brushed her nose into Claire's damp hair smelling her. Like an animal that knew their mate by scent. She wanted to remember Claire's. Nic heard Claire sigh as she pulled her closer to her body.

Claire rolled over and looked at the relaxed face staring back at her. Not sure what she saw in Nic's expression, Claire became concerned when Nic didn't say anything. Was Nic ashamed at what just happened? Surely, she wanted this, as much as Claire did, didn't she? Claire could feel the cold hand of apprehension grip her as Nic just stared at her. *God what have I just done.* A tear started to roll down Claire's face before she could stop it and more followed. Blinking quickly and wiping her eyes, she turned onto her back and faced the ceiling. Why was she crying anyway? Claire took a deep breath and held it to try and stave off more tears. When she released it she sat up and wiped her eyes. She felt the bed shift as Nic sat up and leaned against Claire, wrapping her arms around her.

"Did I do something wrong, Claire?" Nic rested her check on Claire's shoulder and rubbed her arm softly back and forth trying to comfort her.

"God no. Why would you think that? It was the most amazing thing I have ever felt." Nic turned and pulled Claire across her lap cradling her as she rested her forehead against Claire's.

"Then why are you crying?" Nic reached out and brushed another tear from Claire's cheek with her thumb. "I thought maybe I did something wrong or you regretted what just happened."

"Nic, that was the most beautiful thing I've ever felt. I haven't had a lot of experience with women but it was never that freeing, that loving, or that hot."

"You don't regret what happened?" Nic could feel herself relaxing a bit as Claire made her proclamation but she needed to be sure.

"Oh, baby, not at all. I...I...it was unbelievable.

Trust me, I want more." She couldn't hide the smile that crept out behind the tears.

"It was pretty hot, wasn't it?" Nic couldn't help but smile as she remembered how Claire looked when she came. It sent a shiver through her body and she felt herself get wet again.

"You know, I think you need to get rid of this towel Nic." Pushing Nic back, Claire straddled Nic's legs and bent down to kiss her swollen lips.

CHAPTER TWENTY-FIVE

Nic arrived at Claire's house, but she wasn't prepared for what she had to do. In the last couple of days they had become closer, spending lunchtime together, taking Grace on long walks, talking about what Claire would do after the funeral, and when she cleared quarters. Claire actually didn't reveal a lot when it came to her future. She just wasn't sure what she was going to do once everything was finally settled.

Nic knew she was falling in love with Claire. Her body told her as much when she was around her. She struggled not to pull Claire to her every time they were together. She indulged her body's need by caressing Claire's hand when she held it or savoring a stolen kiss when Jordan wasn't looking. Nic made it a point to be on her best behavior around Claire's best friend.

Since their encounter on the back road, Nic had decided that she would court Claire. When she told Claire about her intentions Claire only laughed, and told Nic she hadn't waited this long to be with a woman only to be "respectable". After Nic's declaration, Claire went out of her way to tease Nic. Claire would rub herself against Nic when they lay intertwined on the couch, or she made a point to stare at Nic seductively, her gaze lingering on Nic's lips, as she licked her own. Claire smiled as she watched Nic squirm in torment.

Nic knew Claire was having a lot of fun at her

expense but she didn't mind as long as Claire knew that two could play that game. Nic didn't want to think about what Claire's vagueness about leaving would mean to their relationship, but now it had come full circle and she had to think about it. Nic knocked softly on the front door and stepped down off the stoop as she had done so many times in the recent past. She stood there and thought about the journey she was about to take and she choked up a bit. No, now was not the time to get emotional. She needed to be strong and ready for what lay ahead.

The door swung open and Jordan looked down at Nic. She had never seen Nic in her Khaki dress uniform and looked puzzled for a moment.

"Nic!" she said as she cocked her head as if trying to figure out who the person standing in front of her was. "I'm sorry. I've never seen you in uniform before and you look so formal. Please come in." Jordan closed the door behind her and yelled at Claire, letting her know that Nic was there.

"Jordan, would you mind if Claire and I had a moment alone? I am afraid I have something to tell her and I would like to do it private. I hope you'll understand," Nic said, knowing that Claire would tell Jordan after she left, but she didn't want an audience for the tough moment that lay ahead. Jordan walked down the hall passing Claire and whispering something to her. Claire looked absolutely amazing in her tight jeans and T-shirt and Nic could hardly keep her head where it needed to be. And it wasn't between Claire's legs, Nic reminded herself.

"Nic, don't you look handsome," Claire said as she walked towards Nic. Nic was ramrod straight. Her uniform with its knife creases cut an impressive figure.

She wore it with pride and it showed all the way down to the shiny brass insignia and the chest full of colorful ribbons she wore. She was the model of Marine Corps valor and Claire felt her body clench at the sight. She had never seen Nic looking so official in all of her times with Nic and she liked the look. She admonished herself for thinking of ways to see it on her floor instead of on Nic's sexy body. Claire reached up to kiss Nic, but the Major turned her head. Claire was startled by Nic's reaction, and pulled back before the kiss would have landed on Nic's cheek.

"Nic, what's wrong?" Instantly scared, Claire sat down on the couch as Nic removed her hat and was tucking it into her belt as she sat down next to Claire. Sitting there Nic couldn't help but feel like her world was just about to come crashing down on her. Nic had finally found someone she wanted to spend serious time getting to know and now it was almost over. Her nerves were raw, her guts clenched, and Nic felt herself breaking into a cold sweat. She would rather be back in Iraq than right here, right now. Nic had a duty, and she knew this day would come.

"Claire," Nic said as she took Claire's hands into her own. "They have found Mike, and—"

"Oh God, Nic, don't tell me something else has happened to him, please." Claire slumped against Nic and buried her face into Nic's chest.

Nic felt her chest tighten at the contact, but she continued. She wasn't sure how long she would be able to keep herself from crying, but she had to talk to Claire to tell her how she felt before all hell broke loose and they didn't have time to talk.

"No, I volunteered to bring Mike home. Claire, I need to talk to you before I leave. Once I get back things

will be different for us, you know that don't you?" Nic
asked seriously.

"Wait, why do you have to go bring Mike back,
won't the Marine Corps provide an escort for him?"
Claire was surprised by Nic's offer to escort Mike,
surprised that she would do something so selfless. And
yet maybe she really wasn't surprised. Claire knew she
was the one being selfish. She wanted to spend more time
getting to know Nic and this wouldn't help the process.
She had been thinking of Nic non-stop.

When she wasn't feeling guilty for thinking of Nic
and not Mike, she was wishing she had more time with
her. Claire tried to invent ways of seeing Nic that didn't
look obvious. She had talked to Jordan repeatedly about
the guilt she was feeling and all Jordan did was remind
her that she and Mike had a marriage of convenience
and nothing more.

"Claire, I feel like I owe this to Mike. He was a
good officer and a good friend and now I think I am
falling in love with his wife." Nic's eyes started to tear as
she felt Claire pull her close.

"Claire, please…I just need to do this. I mean—"

"Shh, Nic, I know. I don't know what to say. I love
your sense of honor and duty. No one expects you to do
this. Not me, and certainly not Mike."

"Claire, we need to talk before I leave. I know
when I get back things will be crazy and we won't have
any time to talk about things. I need to tell—"

Nic felt her lips covered by Claire's fingers as
Claire silenced her plea.

"Nic, I don't want you to say something that you
might regret later."

Frustrated, Nic blurted out, "Claire didn't you
hear what I said? I said I am falling in love with you."

Pulling back, Nic looked into Claire's eyes and wasn't sure what she was seeing. Had she been the only one that was feeling this way? Didn't Claire feel it, too, or was she just a brief diversion back into the gay lifestyle for Claire?

Claire's eyes were wide and her hand was pressed to her mouth. She stared at Nic silently.

Steeling herself against the rejection, Nic adjusted her uniform. "Perhaps you're right. It *has* been a stressful time for both of us. I'm sorry, Claire. I need to go. I leave for Dover in half an hour and I need to make sure the arrangements are ready for my arrival."

Turning, she looked at Claire one more time, knowing that it might be the last time she and Claire were alone together.

"Please kiss Grace goodbye for me and I'll let you know when Mike is back."

Without missing a beat, Nic hit the door at almost a full run. She didn't want Claire to see her lose what little control she still had, her eyes betraying her feelings for Claire.

As Nic closed the door she heard Claire whisper, "Nic, please, wait. I—"

CHAPTER TWENTY-SIX

Nic sat in the noisy Marine transport plane, feeling the vibrations from the engines reverberate through her body as it came to a stop on the tarmac. Nic had been briefed about what was expected of her when she landed- how to transport Mike's body, what to do with his effects. They also covered how to handle any issues that might arise from the transportation of the flag draped casket. She had never done this before. It was usually an enlisted member that accompanied a service member's body home, even an officer's. Nic gathered her overnight bag and her briefcase with the documents authorizing her to accept Mike's body on behalf of the Marine Corps and Mike's family.

Nic got off the transport and heard her name called. "Major Caldwell?"

Turning, she saw a young sergeant approach her and snap to a salute. "Major Caldwell."

Saluting back, she looked the young sergeant up and down noticing that either she was getting older or the Marines were promoting grade-schoolers to sergeant. "Sergeant Kelly, is it?"

"Yes ma'am. I am here to take you to briefing and the release. You're here to pick up Capt. Monroe, is that correct?"

"Yes, Sergeant. Lead the way." Dipping her head in a direction that lead away from the still thrumming engines of the transport, she allowed the sergeant to take her overnight bag and escort her to the waiting standard issue military sedan.

"We rarely have an officer escort a body. Was he someone special, Major?"

Nic looked briefly at the young man and then squinted against the sun. Nic slid her sunglasses on. "He was to his family, Sergeant."

"Yes ma'am."

Nic watched as they off-loaded a flag-draped casket from a transport. Looking inside the transport as they passed, she saw several more caskets inside the underbelly of the airplane. This was the part she never saw when her crew was sent home, the pomp and circumstance afforded everyone who died in combat. She watched as the uniformed personnel walked in synchronized step carrying the flag draped coffin to the waiting hearse. She bit her lip and she felt tears start to cloud her vision and a sniffle escaped her.

"Sad, isn't it."

"Excuse me." Wiping her eyes she continued to watch as white-gloved hands passed the casket into the hearse. A salute was rendered, the doors closed, and another hearse took up position to accept another fallen service member. These were the images that the president didn't want the world to see. Each flag draped casket represented a family that had made the ultimate sacrifice for their country. Each casket held a dream that would never be realized, a son or daughter that would never see a parent again, and a life that would never reach its full potential.

The conversation between Nic and Sergeant Kelly was casual and informative as he briefed Nic on what to expect. She had learned that the day Mike came in, they had one of their busiest days, making it tough to get to all the service members in a timely fashion. Losing Mike had put him at the top of the priority list and for that she was grateful.

Nic was escorted into a room and asked to wait as Sergeant Kelly alerted staff of her arrival. While Nic waited, she thought about her last conversation with Claire and how it had gone so wrong. Was Claire right? Was Nic just caught up in the stress of the moment? No. She was falling in love with Claire and she thought that maybe, just maybe, Claire was feeling the same way, too.

"Major Caldwell, good afternoon. I'm Major Latner." A short man in BDU's extended his hand.

"Major Latner."

"I have Capt. Monroe's personal belongings here. Shall we go over them and inventory them?" he asked, motioning Nic to sit down. Major Latner spread the contents of the envelope on the table.

Looking at what was spread before her, she realized she was seeing the only things Mike probably had on him when he died. Nic felt as if she was invading Mike's privacy as she looked at the wallet, dog tags, a box with a Purple Heart, a box with an Air Medal, a crucifix, and an envelope with a red stain smeared across it. Reaching for the envelope, she hesitated as her fingers brushed the stain. It appeared to be blood.

"The envelope contains a letter addressed to a Grace and a Claire. We figured it was to his wife and someone else. We don't usually read them when we find them. We just have to make sure it isn't an important DOD document. Then we put it back. There are also a couple of pictures in it, too."

"It's his daughter and wife," Nic whispered as she touched the envelope again.

"Excuse me?"

"Grace, Grace is Mike's daughter and Claire is his wife." Nic could feel the tears fall as she realized that Mike would never see his little girl again. She thought about her own crew as she caressed the envelope and tucked it inside her jacket. Had their families received similar items from their loved ones? Had someone handed them a packet of belongings like they were delivering the mail?

"Oh. Well, he wrote them letters. Major, you can put that back in here if you like."

"No, if you don't mind I would like to personally deliver this," she said, patting her chest where the letter lay protected. "I know his wife and daughter and I would like to make sure someone who cares delivers it. We can put everything else in there though." Nic handed Major Latner the rest of Mike's personal things and watched as he closed the envelope.

"Here is a flag for the casket. Now, if you will sign for everything, I will take you to Capt. Monroe and we can load him up for transport."

Nic was taken to a row of caskets and watched as they verified the tag on the casket with the label on the packet. They scanned both labels and then handed her the packet.

"Major Latner? Could you please open the casket?"

"Major Caldwell you can't be serious. I don't recommend that you or his family view Capt. Monroe's remains. He took a lot of damage and he shouldn't have an open casket funeral."

"Sir, I need to make sure that this is Capt. Monroe. Trust me, I don't want to do it but I think, considering the circumstances, we need to make sure it is Capt.

Monroe."

"Major..."

"Please, Major Latner. I want to be able to tell his family that it is him."

"If you feel you must."

Motioning to an enlisted man, Major Latner unscrewed the lid of the casket and lifted it enough so Nic could look inside. Inside was Mike's body, his face bruised with a long stitched wound across it. He wore the dress blue uniform jacket of a Marine Corps officer, a chest full of medals, his purple heart and a bronze star the latest additions to his awards, and his blue slacks finishing off his appearance. Nic nodded to the enlisted man and watched as they ratcheted down the casket lid for the final time.

"We clean them up, get a uniform custom made, and then add all of his ribbons and medals. Added, of course, are his Purple Heart and Air Medal. You'll notice that we also provide one of each for his family. Well, Major, if you're satisfied we will load him for transport."

Nodding, Nic set her briefcase and overnight bag down as she watched the Major call over six Marines to carry Mike to the waiting SUV. With military precision and bearing, each Marine addressed the casket and upon command reached down slowly and lifted Mike's casket chest high. Nic could feel her throat tighten as she snapped to attention and slowly raised her right hand in salute as they loaded Mike into the SUV. Eyes forward, she watched as each member of the detail passed the casket forward and into the vehicle. Slowly, she lowered her salute as the doors to the SUV closed and the detail was dismissed. She grabbed her and Mike's belongings, thanked Major Latner and made her way to the waiting vehicle.

On her way to the airport, she thought about whether she should tell Claire she had requested to see, Mike's body. She had wanted to make sure that it was him. She didn't want Claire to have to endure any more problems just in case the military made another mistake and had given her someone else's body by accident. She was glad she had checked, and that she could tell Claire with no doubt it was him.

When they reached the smaller transport plane that would take them almost all the way to San Diego, Nic watched as the same process started all over again as they took the casket and loaded it onto the plane. Once inside, Nic stowed her belongings under the webbing under her seat and took the flag out of its protective case. Laying the flag on the casket, she began to unfurl it. Placing the stars at the head and over Mike's left shoulder. She opened the flag to its full width and length and then began the process of draping the casket.

"Ma'am, would you like me to do that for you?" asked a private who was moving towards her.

"No Private, thank you. I think I can manage," Nic said as she folded one corner down and over and secured it in place. Standing, Nic snapped to attention and saluted the flag draped casket. She watched out of the corner of her eye as several other service members snapped to attention and saluted. Lowering her salute, she noticed the other service members still at attention.

"At ease." Nic gave the other service members a small smile. "Thank you."

Each one nodded and went back to their duties as Nic sat down and tried to get comfortable in the web seating.

"Major, you can sit in the cabin. We have seating

up there," said a young service member.

"Thank you, but here is fine," Nic said as she looked at Mike's casket. "I'll be fine."

Nic wasn't sure if the crew understood or not, but she didn't want to leave Mike's body. She had said she would escort it and that was exactly what she would do. Taking her service cap off, a member of the crew brought a blanket out to Nic and told her that it would get pretty cold when they got to altitude.

Nick reached into her jacket pocket and pulled out the envelope she had tucked inside for safe keeping. Looking at the blood smear across it, she wondered if Mike had suffered. What were his last thoughts? Were they of Grace and Claire or were they on survival? Flipping the envelope over three pictures slid out, one of Grace, one of Mike and Grace and one of Mike and a guy Nic didn't recognize. Nic picked up the two pictures of Grace and smiled as she looked at a happy little girl and a happy dad with his daughter. Nic smiled as she placed the two pictures back in the envelope. Then she gave the last one a hard look. Mike and the guy were in civilian clothes and were in a "buddy pose", the kind that guys goofing around took when they had too much to drink. Something struck Nic as odd as she continued to look at the photo of the two men. Was he a fellow officer or perhaps a contract civilian that worked over in Iraq?

Nic studied the picture wondering why Mike had put this one with his pictures of Grace. Something didn't seem right, but Mike was gone and no one could answer that question except the guy in the picture. Nic slid the picture into her outer jacket pocket and the envelope with the letter and pictures of Grace into her inside pocket for safe keeping. Nic wondered why Mike didn't have any pictures of Claire in his personal possessions. Even if he were just "keeping up appearances", he should have had at least one picture of his wife.

Looking at the casket she thought about Mike and the life he was able to enjoy before he died. Mike had everything she wanted in life, a military career, a beautiful wife and daughter, and he was on the fast track to promotion with his two tours in Iraq. What had she spent the last ten years of her life for? She couldn't marry, she would never have what Mike had, and she almost gave her life for what? "Don't ask, don't tell" really meant don't be happy, don't be who you really are. She was here and Mike was lying in a casket and come to find out he was gay, too.

Nic wanted what Mike had, and to get it she had to make a choice. She sighed as she thought of Claire, absently stroking the letter through her jacket pocket. Nic hadn't planned on falling in love with Claire. She had just been asked to help out a friend's family, but it had happened. As long as Nic was a Marine, she couldn't offer Claire anything. Heck, she couldn't offer herself a shot at happiness for that matter. They had talked about the future but in vague terms, neither wanting to ask the real question—what if? Nic knew Claire would never ask her to get out for her sake. Claire was selfless when it came to someone else's happiness. No, Claire wasn't that type of person, which is why Nic had fallen in love with her. Now Nic just needed to find out if Claire loved her. If she did, Nic had to get out of the military, plain and simple.

CHAPTER TWENTY-SEVEN

Claire sat on the front porch watching Grace play on the lawn. Her mind wandered back to the day Nic left. Nic had told her she loved her, and all Claire could think to do was chalk it up to stress. *God how stupid could I be?* Why hadn't she just told Nic the truth? That she was falling in love with her, too. Because Nic had her whole career ahead of her, and Claire couldn't be part of that journey with her and she knew it. She wasn't going to ask Nic to give up everything she worked so hard for just for her. She wasn't going to take advantage of Nic's feelings. As soon as she buried Mike, she had thirty days to clear quarters and start her new life and Nic couldn't be part of that life. No, she had been right not to tell Nic how she felt. Claire heard the door shut behind her and turned to see Jordan offering her a cup of coffee.

"Hey you. Whatcha thinking about?"

"Hey Jor. Nothing." Sipping her coffee, Claire stared at Grace as she somersaulted on the lawn, giggling.

"How come I don't believe you, kitten?"

"Because you know me so well?"

Jordan put an arm around Claire's shoulders and pulled her close. "What's wrong sweetie? Is it Nic?"

Claire laid her head on her friend's shoulder and shrugged. "I don't know. I think I might have screwed things up."

Jordan thought back to the day Nic went to look for Claire on her bike. "I don't think you can get rid of tall, dark and gorgeous that easily. But it must have been pretty bad if you think she's gone. What did you say?"

Claire rehashed the conversation she had with Nic. Thinking about it only succeeded in making her feel worse. Claire started to tear up at how she had downplayed Nic's revelation that she was in love with her.

"I was so callous, Jordan. I completely dismissed her feelings," Claire said, staring at her hands.

"Well, maybe you're scared, kitten."

"What do mean? Scared of what?"

"Let me ask you this. Do you like her?"

"Of course. She's wonderful, smart, sexy as hell and let's not forget she looks hot in that uniform. What's not to like? Then there is Grace to think about, Nic is great with Grace. You should have seen them the night Nic came to tell me about the Marine Corps losing Mike's body. I found her asleep with Grace in the rocking chair. They were so cute together. Like mother and child. Besides, she loves Grace and Grace loves her. Oh Jordan, what am I going to do?" Claire plucked a piece of grass growing between the stones and rolled it absently between her fingers.

"Okay, so don't answer this right away, but is it possible that you are falling in love with her, too? Now, answer honestly. It's just you and me here."

Claire closed her eyes and started to rub her temples. Hadn't she just told herself that she thought she was falling for Nic? So why was it so hard to admit it out loud? It wasn't like Jordan was going to tell her little secrets. Even if she did, what did it matter now that Mike was gone and soon, Nic would be too?

"You're right, I am scared, Jor." She was scared Nic would pick the military over her. Scared that if she let Nic know how she really felt that it wouldn't really matter to her. Hadn't Mike chosen his career over his family? Not that what she wanted with Nic was the same as what she had with Mike. Convenience versus love, the two things couldn't be more different than heaven and hell.

"Do you love her, Claire?"

"Yeah, I do. And I know she has a career here and that I can't be part of that. So if I tell her how I feel, I'm just opening myself up to be hurt." Claire buried her face in her crossed arms and started to cry.

"Aw, sweetie."

"Thank you, Private. I appreciate the loan of the phone," Nic said passing the cell phone back to the private who had loaned it to her when they landed to refuel.

"No luck, Major?"

"No. I guess the Captain's wife is out. I left a message. Thanks."

Nic had hoped to talk to Claire and at least let her know that she had something important to talk to her about when she returned. Instead, she got Claire's voice mail and ended up leaving a message that only said something about an important change in Nic's life. She sighed and rested her head against the wall for a moment, thinking about all that needed to be done when she arrived back on base.

She needed to talk to her commander about her decision, start looking for a job, and find where she wanted to live. She decided that she would stay in the Marine Corps Reserve so that some money continued to come in while she figured out what to do next. She had a friend who taught counter-terrorism classes at the Naval Postgraduate School in Monterey, California. He had been after her for some time to consider teaching there. Maybe now was the time. Her background and experience made her a good fit for the school and she loved the area. San Diego was fine for a while, but it took a special someone to be able to handle all that traffic.

Finally, Nic felt like her life had some direction. She realized she had felt like a ship without a rudder, floundering while her body healed and she waited for the military to finally decide what to do with her, and she hated it. Now she was in control. Nic continued her mental list of all the things she needed to do when she got back. She knew what she wanted and she knew who she wanted to be with. Looking in her briefcase, she grabbed her dead cell phone and tapped on the keys. God, how could she have been so forgetful and not charged the darn thing?

All she wanted to do was to call Claire and tell her the news, and ask her if she wanted to be part of it. *Three more hours.* Three more hours and she would start a new path that, hopefully, included Claire and Grace. *What if she doesn't want me?* She couldn't silence the nagging voice. She knew she needed to prepare herself for that possibility. Claire hadn't exactly seemed happy to hear Nic's revelation the last time they had talked. Closing her eyes and resting her head against the aircraft, she felt her chest tighten. *What will I do if Claire has different plans?* Nic felt her elation darken as she thought about all the possibilities. Now that she was finally taking control over her life again, she had to admit to herself that she wasn't in control of the one thing she wanted most, Claire.

"Major, we're ready for take off. Can I get you anything before we close the hatch?"

"No, Private, but thanks," Nic said, knowing he couldn't get her the one thing she really needed.

Nodding, the young serviceman walked back and pushed the button that would shut the huge hydraulic door and move Nic closer to her final destination.

CHAPTER TWENTY-EIGHT

"Ma'am. Major Caldwell?" Nic felt someone shaking her shoulder as she jerked awake.

"Sorry ma'am, but we are on our final approach to the base and you need to buckle-up."

Nic couldn't believe that she had fallen asleep in the oversized mixer and looking down, she noticed she was covered in the blanket the private had given her earlier.

"Thanks, Private," Nic mumbled as she folded the blanket and smoothed her uniform.

"Ma'am, the funeral detail will be waiting when we land. Is there anything else you need?"

"No. Please thank the crew for me and thank you for the use of the phone and the blanket." Nic smiled as she made sure her things were stowed for landing.

"Ma'am, I just want to say that Captain Monroe's family was lucky to have you as a friend, seeing that you came all this way to bring him home. I hope if something happens to me, someone will do the same for my family."

"Private, nothing is going to happen to you so you don't have to worry. But trust me, if something happens to you, there will be someone just like me waiting to take you home. Understand Marine?" Nic's eyes started to water as she reached down and grabbed her service cap. "Besides, you don't have my permission to die,

Private," she said as she tucked a stray strand of hair back in place.

"Yes ma'am."

"Good, now that we have an understanding, let's get Captain Monroe home to his family."

"Yes ma'am."

Nic watched as the private strapped himself into his own seat. He couldn't have been much younger that the crew chief she lost in her helicopter accident. Her throat tightened as she thought about the men and their families. Looking down at the flag draped casket, she knew that those feelings would be with her every time she saw this very image.

As the aircraft rolled to a stop Nic gathered her briefcase and overnight bag and set them in the seat next to her. Standing, she took up position at the head of the casket and watched as the back door was lowered. Waiting for them at the end of the plane was a full military funeral detail in dress uniform. Slowly, Nic raised her salute as the honor guard entered the bay of the plane. Each member walked in synchronized step moving into position next to the casket. Upon command, they lifted Mike's body up and slowly moved him towards the back of the plane. Nic followed the procession and, on reaching the tarmac, noticed that the crew of the plane had disembarked and was standing at attention, saluting their fellow soldier. The flag draped casket was passed slowly into the hearse and, as the doors shut, each service member slowly dropped their salute. Nic could hear a few sniffles as she reached up to wipe her own eyes. Now it was real, now she had to tell Claire that Mike was back for good.

Nic stood there for a moment looking at the stars and stripes peeking through the back window of the hearse. Claire could get real closure now that Mike's funeral could be arranged. Nic had never gotten that closure for herself. For a time, she had half expected to see her crew come walking through the door any minute to tell her it was all a really bad joke, but it never happened. Her scars were real, and her pain was real. It wasn't until she visited Arlington and saw the headstones of a few of her crewmen that she knew it was real. Nic choked back her tears. Now came the hard part. The family, the funeral, the finality.

"Major Caldwell, when you're ready." The funeral director motioned to the hearse.

"Of course." Nic turned and nodded to the private who had lingered a moment longer.

"Good night, Private and good luck."

"You, too, Major Caldwell." Standing straight, the young man saluted smartly.

Shaking her head, Nic smiled and returned the salute. Then she got into the hearse.

CHAPTER TWENTY-NINE

Claire dried herself off as she stood in front of the bathroom mirror. Nic was due back anytime and she was surprised she hadn't heard from her. Mike's family had called and informed Claire that they had arrived and were staying at a local hotel. They had brought everyone and there was no way they could stay at Claire's, but she had offered anyway. Luckily, they had already made the hotel arrangements when Claire had called the first time to inform them of Mike's death. Claire and Mike's mom got along, but they would never be "shopping buddies" as Mike's mom liked to call Gail, Claire's sister-in-law. It was just as well. Claire wasn't much of a shopper, and the highlight of her day didn't involve finding the best deal on Monteau's clearance rack.

Dressing, Claire poked her head out the bathroom door. "Hey Jordan, did my phone ring while I was in the shower?"

"Nope. I didn't hear it. Did you hear it Gracie?"

Claire heard a little voice echo Jordan's negative answer and then a squeal of delight as Jordan and Grace started wrestling on the floor again. Claire was thankful Jordan had decided to come uninvited. She was a good diversion for Grace as Claire made the arrangements to clear housing. Walking back into her bedroom, Claire sidestepped half-full boxes of Mike's stuff. She had started to separate his things into items that she thought her mother-in-law might like to take with her when she left and other stuff that she would give to the local thrift shop on base. Looking around, she couldn't see her cell phone so she started a mad hunt for her purse, hopeful that it was in there and not somewhere Grace had hidden it.

"Hey, have you two seen my purse? I need to check my cell phone."

"It was on the counter last time I saw it," Jordan said as she wrestled Grace to the floor, the three year old squealing all the way down.

"Yeah, it was on the counter last time I saw it," Grace said as she licked Jordan's face.

"Yuk. Where did you learn that?" Jordan said as she wiped her face with her sleeve.

"It's a cow lick, silly, and I knew you would get off me if I did that. Ha!" Grace said as she scrambled out from under Jordan and ran to her room.

"Yuk. Who taught her that, gross," Jordan said, still wiping her face as she went into the kitchen to find Claire.

Claire had her cell phone to her ear and a finger to her mouth motioning Jordan to be quiet. A look of concern etched its way across Claire's face as she lowered the phone and looked at Jordan.

"That was Nic. It seems something's happened to her and she needs to talk to me. Jordan, what do you think that means? Oh God, I bet she's being shipped overseas again, or maybe she's being reassigned somewhere else! Shit."

Claire flung herself onto the couch and covered her eyes with her arm. It was the worst news possible. First Mike, now Nic. What else could happen? Claire felt her chest tighten and a knot grow in her throat as she started to cry.

"Wait, wait, wait. You don't know what that means so don't jump to anything just yet. Come on. What else did she say?"

"She said she needed to talk to me, and if she didn't hear back from me, then she understood."

Claire ran back into the kitchen and grabbed her phone.

"What are you doing?"

"Checking to see what time Nic called. Shit."

Sliding to the floor, tears trailed down Claire's face as she closed her eyes tight, trying to shut out the world. As she took a shuddered breath, she felt Jordan sit next to her wrapping her arms around her.

"When did she call?"

"Five hours ago, five fucking hours ago. Damn it! I'm sure she thinks I don't want to talk to her now. She said they were three hours out and that I should call her, then. Oh, God."

Claire rocked back and forth and tried to figure out what to do next. *Why didn't I have my cell phone with me?* She berated herself repeatedly for not having the annoying little device. Burying her head in her hands, she began to cry.

"Why? Why? Why?" Claire was sobbing now. "Jordan, what am I going to do?"

"Look, it isn't the end of the world. We can try to give her a call and tell her we didn't get the message. Here, give me the phone and let's try, okay?"

Handing Jordan the phone, Claire sat transfixed as Jordan dialed Nic's number. Claire could hear the ringing of the phone as Jordan held it away from her face. Claire relaxed as she heard Nic's voice.

"Claire, it's her answering machine. Do you want

me to leave a message?"

Claire felt like someone had punched her in the stomach. Obviously, Nic didn't want to talk to her or she would have seen the number and picked up. Crestfallen, Claire picked herself up off the floor and shook her head no.

"No, I'm sure she can see my number on her phone. She knows it's me and doesn't want to talk to me. Forget it."

Claire sprawled herself on the couch flinging her arm over her face. Tears slowly crept from beneath the tightly closed eyes and Claire could no longer stop them from falling. *What will I do now?* Why hadn't she just told Nic how she felt? Nic made her feel loved, wanted, and special. No one had ever made her feel that way, not her first girlfriend, not Carole in college, and especially not Mike. Nic was different. Nic made her tingle. She made her giddy. She knew it sounded stupid, but she liked feeling giddy. Claire felt the couch lower with Jordan's weight as she lay next to Claire and wrapped her arms around her.

"It will be alright, kitten. I just know it," Jordan whispered.

CHAPTER THIRTY

Nic looked down at her watch and noted the time, midnight. All she wanted was to take off her uniform, grab a cold beer, a hot shower, and not necessarily in that order. Tossing her keys on the counter, her briefcase on the couch, and her hat on the hanger she started to unbutton her uniform jacket. It had been a long forty-eight hours and she was glad to finally be home. If she had been able to see Claire, it would have been a bonus night. After hanging her jacket in the closet, Nic made her way into the tiny kitchen and opened the door. Thirst or hunger. Which pang would she feed first. Pulling a beer from the fridge, she answered that question. She could eat later. Right now, she needed to relax. She let the amber liquid slide down her throat feeling its relaxing effects almost immediately. It was time to make plans for the future and her departure from the Marine Corps was first on her agenda. The flashing red light of her answering machine caught her eye as she tossed the empty bottle into the trash.

"Major Caldwell, this is Father O'Rielly. Can you give me a call when you get in? Thanks."

"Beep"

"Major, this is Sergeant Ross, just checking in to see how your flight was. Let me know when you'll be in the office and I'll have your coffee waiting."

Nic could hear Sergeant Ross chuckling in the

background as he hung up the phone.

There weren't anymore messages. Claire hadn't called. *Damn it.* Nic felt her heart sink. She had been wrong about Claire's feelings for her. How could she have been so wrong about Claire? Maybe she was just transferring her feeling for Mike to Nic. It probably wasn't unusual. They had warned her about families becoming too dependent on the person assigned to help them when their loved one died. This was different, way different.

She needed to move on with her life. But how could she do it without Claire?

CHAPTER THIRTY-ONE

The next few days were a blur for Claire with all the arrangements she had to make and with family members arriving from out of state. She had little time to wonder where Nic had gone. Sitting at the funeral home for the vigil, she greeted each person as they arrived to pay their respects to Mike. Officers and enlisted alike told her stories of how Mike had either helped them get through some rough patch or made them laugh with funny stories of Grace. However, there was one person that never showed and Claire wished Nic would come so she could at least explain why she hadn't called. She thought about calling Nic but every time she made her way to the phone something always came up.

Claire watched the door and shook her head when Jordan leaned over and whispered, "Still no tall, dark and handsome?"

"No, I'm afraid not. What am I going to do, Jordan? I need to talk to her, and explain things. Surely it can't end like this? I don't want it to end." Tears rolled down Claire's face as she pleaded her case to her best friend.

"I know, sweetie, I know."

Just then, Mike's mom came in, walked to the casket and crossed herself. She looked at Claire and seeing that Claire was crying, she started to cry herself.

"Don't worry, honey, it will be alright. You have

lots of family that want to help. It will be all right. Trust me." Patting Claire's hand, she took out a tissue from between her breasts and handed it to Claire.

"Thanks, mom. I think I need to get some fresh air and freshen up. You don't mind sitting here for a while do you?"

"No, not at all, hon. You go and I'll sit with Mike. Besides, I need to say a few prayers. The more prayers, the quicker to heaven," she said with a sad smile as she knelt down on the prayer bench.

"Jordan, can you come with me?"

"Sure, hon."

Outside in the fresh, warm sun, Claire closed her eyes and waited, and waited, and waited.

"Claire, what's wrong?"

"Nothing. Hear that?"

"Hear what? I don't hear anything."

"Exactly. It's quiet, the only noise is those birds singing. I'm sorry, Jordan. I guess I should be thankful that so many people have come to pay their respects, but I have to be honest. I'm on overload and there is only one thing I can really think about right now. Okay two things, Grace and Nic."

"Do you want to talk about it?"

"No. And I'm not gonna call and bother her. I figure she saw that it was me calling her the other night and she didn't answer so that sends a pretty strong message, wouldn't you say?"

"Maybe, but sometimes you really should talk to someone face-to-face. I mean with all the technology it's easy to think everyone is right at your fingertips." Jordan held her hands up as if she was going to squeeze Claire's breast.

"Knock it off, silly."

"Look, why don't you wait until all of this is over and then you two can talk. I mean she went and escorted Mike all the way from the east coast to here. I can't imagine she would tell you she loved you and then drop you like a hot potato, can you?"

"I screwed up and now I am paying for it. God, how could I have been so stupid?"

Claire wondered if she would even get a chance to talk to the officer before Nic left, assuming that was what Nic was referring to in the message she had left. For all she knew, Nic might have shipped out already. Claire fervently hoped that wasn't true. She needed to talk to Nic, even if it didn't change anything. Nic deserved to know how she really felt about her.

"Claire, Jordan, how are you ladies holding up?" Father O'Reilly approached the two women and gave them both a warm embrace. Turning towards Claire he said, "How is Grace, my dear?"

"She's fine Father, a little overwhelmed I think, but it will all be over soon. Then the adjustment starts."

"Well, she has a fine mother who I know will help her through it all. I just stopped by to make sure everything was in order for tomorrow's funeral. So if you will excuse me." Kissing Claire on the cheek, Father O'Reilly turned to go into the church.

"Uh Father, can I talk to you for a minute? Jordan you don't mind, do you?"

"No. I need to freshen up myself. See you inside. Bye Father, see you tomorrow."

"What's wrong, Claire? I can see you seem troubled. Is it Michael's mother? Would you like me to talk to her?"

"No Father. It's Nic. Have you seen her?" Claire looked down at her hands that were twisting a handkerchief. "I haven't seen her since before she left to pick up Mike."

"I spoke to her briefly once after she returned but that's been all. Odd she hasn't been by to see you. Well, perhaps she knows you have lots of family and the last thing you need is someone else hanging around." Father O'Reilly smiled warmly as he grasped Claire's hands. "What is really bothering you, Claire?"

"Thank God! Sorry Father, I was afraid she'd been shipped out."

Claire began to cry as Father O'Reilly led her to a nearby bench and sat down with her, putting a strong arm around her shoulders.

"There, there Claire. Whatever has happened between you two surely can't be that bad. Perhaps it's a simple misunderstanding," the priest said.

Claire began to tell the priest about the conversation she had had with Nic just before she left for the airport, about the missed message Nic had left and about the fact that she hadn't called Nic back until it was too late. Now Nic thought she didn't want to talk to her because Nic didn't answer her phone when she called.

"Claire, what makes you think it is too late? Sometimes things happen for a reason and perhaps this has helped you to understand how you really feel about Nic. Before Nic left perhaps you weren't ready to think of a life that included her, because of Nic's career in the military, or perhaps because of what Mike's death really means to you. You can finally live your own life, if you choose." Claire looked up into the wrinkled face that seemed to smile when no smile was there. "But shouldn't you let Nic decide what is good for her, if she loves you like she said she does? Nic will make the right choices. If not, then God has other plans for you two. But, I think you owe it to Nic to tell her how you really feel, don't you?

"Yes but..."

"No, Claire, no buts. Promise me that you will talk to her. Promise?" Now the priest was smiling and his eyes twinkled.

"I will, Father. I promise."

"Good. Now if you will excuse me, I need to take care of something for tomorrow." Reaching down he kissed Claire's cheek and left her to sit in the sun.

Claire closed her eyes and ran her fingers through her hair, the warmth of the day feeling good to her tired body. She thought about Nic and wondered where she was. She needed to talk to her, to set everything straight and get on with her life one way or the other.

CHAPTER THIRTY-TWO

Nic sat at her desk finishing a stack of paperwork that had accumulated while she was gone. Forty-eight hours and someone would think all hell broke loose while she was gone. She knew she would be glad when she was done with this job and out of the Marine Corps. But for now she had a job to do and, until she had a date leaving military service, nothing was a guarantee. She had spent a good portion of the last couple of days talking to her friend at the Naval Post Graduate School in Monterey. To her surprise, they still needed an anti-terrorism expert. After quizzing him about the surrounding area and the cost of living, she told him she would need a day or two to think about it but if the offer was still open he could expect to see her resume, which she had faxed to him that morning.

Nic sat at her desk thinking about Claire and how she was doing. She missed her, missed her a lot, and it was all she could do not to call her, but Claire had decided for them when she didn't call Nic back. Nic did a lot of things when she was interested in a woman but chase her wasn't one of them. Although if she *was* going to chase, Claire would be worth it.

Nic's phone buzzed. "Major, Father O'Reilly is here to see you. Shall I send him in?"

"Of course Sergeant. Please send him in."

Nic stood up and waited for the priest to come

in.

"Good Afternoon, Father. Shouldn't you be at the church or with Mike's family or something? I mean, not that I'm not glad to see you but I figured you would be needed somewhere else right now." She motioned to the seat in front of her desk as she spoke.

"Well, actually Nic, I am on a mission, so to speak." Smiling, the priest declined the coffee Nic offered.

Nic sat back in her seat and steepled her hands in front of her.

"Okay, so what brings you to my neck of the woods, Father?"

"Claire Monroe."

"Claire? Is something wrong? Is she okay?" Nic began to rise from her seat but the priest motioned her down and back into it.

"Yes, but it seems she is having a problem, Nic, and perhaps you can help her?"

"Well, I'll do what I can Father, but at this point I don't think she needs my help anymore."

"On the contrary, it seems there was some miscommunication recently and she is rather upset over it."

"Father, I don't think I follow you," Nic said, hoping this conversation wasn't going where she thought it was going.

"Nic, I think you do. I had a rather long conversation with Claire today. She was very distraught—"

"Father, she just lost her husband so she is going to be distraught...."

"Nic, do you remember when I told you that you and Claire had more in common than you might think? Well, I knew about Mike and Claire's relationship."

Father O'Reilly waited while his words sunk in.

"Let me get this straight. You knew about the Monroe's marriage?" Nic couldn't believe what she was hearing. Father O'Reilly had known all along that Mike and Claire were gay.

"Yes."

"But you're an officer and ..."

Cutting Nic off again, he said, "I wore a collar long before I wore camouflage Nic, and what is said in the sanctity of the church beats any "don't ask, don't tell" policy."

Stunned, Nic sat staring at the priest. She couldn't believe what she was hearing. Never had she been in a situation like this where a high ranking officer choose to overlook something so...so egregious.

"Nic, if I didn't keep the sanctity of the church what use would I be to my parishioners? I love my country, I love my parishioners, but most of all, I love my God and I don't judge my flock. That isn't my job. When Mike came to me and confessed in confessional, I couldn't judge him. He told me he had left that lifestyle behind, and I chose to believe him."

Nic thought about the picture she had found in Mike's possessions. She would never be the one to tell the priest that Mike might have lied, or maybe he didn't lie. Maybe he thought he had, but it was just too hard. Either way, it wasn't her job. Like the priest she had a duty, too, and that was to keep an old friend's secrets.

"I understand. So why are you here?"

"On behalf of a friend. You."

"Okay, now I am confused. I didn't call you, Father."

"As I said earlier, I spoke with a very distraught Claire. I hope you don't mind, but she confided in me."

"Father, I am not sure I like where this is going. Didn't you just say that you're under some sort of order not to divulge private matters discussed with you?"

"Well yes and no. Claire isn't Catholic and it wasn't said in the church."

"But you're a man of the cloth, right?"

"Minor technicality, but yes."

Nic needed to stop the conversation. If he told her what she thought he was going to say, she could be court-martialed at worst, or be given a dishonorable discharge at best.

"Look, Father I can explain…" Nic got up and closed the door that led to Sergeant Ross's desk and turned to face Father O'Reilly. "I'm not sure how to say this but…"

"Stop, Nic. I'm not here to accuse you of anything so before you say anything else, please sit down and listen to me."

Nic felt a cold sweat break out across her body. Sitting down, she took a deep breath and held it as she tried to stop from blacking out. Never before had she imagined being caught and never by a Chaplain or another officer. She had always been discreet and now her whole career was flashing before her eyes.

"Nic, deep breaths. Trust me on this okay? Good, nice deep breaths Nic. Relax. Are you okay?"

Nodding, Nic looked down at her hands and wished she was anywhere else but there.

"Nic, I had a long conversation with Claire, and before you say anything, remember I am here as a friend. It seems that you two have had some miscommunication in the past few days. All I am going to say is that I think you need to go and see her now. She is at the church until around eight tonight. I have asked her to come to the office right after that to talk about tomorrow. I want you to be there. That's an order. You don't have to say anything but I want you to listen. You owe her that."

Without another word Father O'Reilly got up and turned to leave. "See you tomorrow at the funeral."

Nic sat at her desk, her hands covering her mouth. Did Father O'Reilly just give her a pass on what he knew about her and Claire? Wait, did he just plan a clandestine meeting for her with Claire? Nic slumped back against her chair, suddenly spent. One minute she was watching her career pass before her eyes, and the next she was being ordered to meet another woman at the church rectory.

CHAPTER THIRTY-THREE

Claire looked at her watch. A few minutes before eight. As she sat there she was grateful for the few minutes alone to gather her thoughts. It seemed she had been on autopilot the whole time and rarely had a minute to herself. Grace had gone home with Jordan and Mike's mom. They were glad for a small diversion, too. Everyone was on their best behavior, but it was trying at times. Never knowing what to say to anyone or how to respond when they offered their condolences made it hard to hold even a small conversation. Claire fidgeted as she looked back down at her watch. *He had said eight hadn't he,* she thought. She heard the door handle jiggle as it was turned and stood up to greet Father O'Reilly. But it wasn't Father O'Reilly that came through the door.

"Hi, I guess you weren't expecting me, were you?" Nic said softly, her eyes searching Claire's for answers.

"No, not unless the big thing you needed to tell me is that you're joining the priesthood," Claire said as she stepped closer to Nic.

"Naw, I don't think they would take me. Besides, I'm not Catholic, at least not anymore." Smiling, Nic grabbed one of Claire's hands and was surprised when she didn't pull it back. Moving towards the chairs, she sat Claire in one and took the other that faced her.

"How have you been?" Nic couldn't take her eyes off Claire's lips as she caressed the hand she still held.

"Okay. Better now."

"I understand you needed to talk to me."

Before Claire could say anything else Nic was standing over her, her face being held in Nic's hands. Leaning down, Nic slowly kissed Claire as she pulled her to her feet.

"I am so sorry, Claire. Please forgive me," Nic whispered between kisses.

"What, wait." Claire stopped Nic and gently pushed her back. "What do you have to be sorry for? I'm the one that screwed up and didn't tell you how I felt. I'm the one that should be apologizing to you. Oh Nic…" Claire buried her head on Nic's shoulder as Nic wrapped her arms around her. "I tried to call you and you didn't pick up. I didn't know you called, I swear, or I would have called you right back. I would never have waited so long to call you back but…"

"Shhh." Nic put her finger over Claire's mouth.

"It's okay. I think I understand what happened. However, can you forgive me? My pride wouldn't let me call you. I thought you didn't want to be with me after I told you I was falling in love with you. When you didn't call me back I just figured you didn't want me."

"Oh God Nick, are you kidding? I love you." Kissing Nic again Claire pulled back and, holding Nic's face in her hands, said it again. "I love you. I think I have from the minute I saw you. Is that bad? I mean with only just losing Mike and falling in love with you. Do you think badly of me?"

"I am guilty of the same, my love. We don't get to choose when love finds us. Maybe we should just be happy that it did."

CHAPTER THIRTY-FOUR

It took a month to leave San Diego. It had taken longer than she had hoped for Claire to clear quarters in San Diego, but that had given her the time necessary to expedite her own depature from the military and move to the Reserve Corps. Three months later, Nic couldn't be happier. They were together in Monterey and Nic was getting ready to start a new job with the Naval Post Graduate School. Once they had decided to take their relationship to the next level and Nic left the military, it became easier.

"Nickie, Nickie," Grace said as she ran to the back of the moving truck.

Jumping down, Nic picked up Grace and swung her around. "Hi honey. What's up?"

"Mommy said I have to ask you if I can have this now." Graced opened her hands showing Nic a roll of candy.

"She did, did she?"

"Yep. She said you're the boss," Grace said giggling as Nic tickled her.

"Okay, but you can only have one. You'll spoil your lunch if you eat more," Nic said as she set Grace on the ground. Nic looked up to see Claire watching her from the fence.

"I'm the boss huh?" Nic said as she closed the distance between her and Claire, wrapping her arms around her.

"Well, she has to get used to having two mommies now, doesn't she?" Claire questioned as she kissed Nic lightly on the neck.

"If you keep that up I'm gonna put Grace down for a nap and show you who the boss really is," Nic whispered.

"Excuse me. Where do you want this dresser," a burley man asked as he wheeled a dresser down the trailer's loading ramp.

"Guess I better get back to work," Nic said, a little embarrassed at being caught kissing Claire.

"Yeah, I guess you better. Come on Grace. Let's go make lunch." Claire reached up and gave Nic a peck on the cheek. "See you in a few minutes."

"Okay. I love you."

"I love you, too, baby."

Nic smiled as she watched her new family go into the house. She knew tomorrow was filled with a promise she never thought she would have.

About the Author

Isabella lives in California with her wife and three sons. She works for two non-profits, and speaks at high schools and universities on current issuses facing the LGBT community. She likes traveling with her wife, riding her motorcycle and spending time with her family.

She is a member of Gold Crown Literary Society, Romance Writers of America. She has written several short stories, and is now working on her next novel.

CPSIA information can be obtained at www.ICGtesting.com
Printed in the USA
LVOW041234280712

291971LV00001B/139/P